THE SECRET
OF
GUMBO GROVE

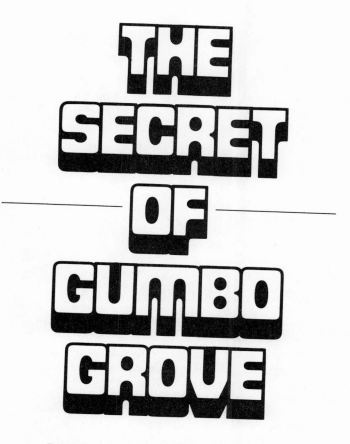

THE SECRET OF GUMBO GROVE

BY ELEANORA E. TATE

Franklin Watts / 1987 / New York / Toronto

Library of Congress Cataloging-in-Publication Data

Tate, Eleanora E.
The secret of Gumbo Grove.

Summary: While helping restore the cemetery of
the old Baptist church, eleven-year-old Raisin
solves the mystery surrounding the founding of her
home town and gains pride in her family's past.
[1. Afro-Americans—Fiction. 2. South Carolina—
Fiction. 3. Mystery and detective stories] I. Title.
PZ7.T21117se 1987   [Fic]   86-26742
ISBN 0-531-10298-X

To Zack,
for bringing me to South Carolina,

and to the
late Michael Earl Vereen
and Lila Lee McKnight
for showing me its beauty

THE SECRET
OF
GUMBO GROVE

1

Big Boy stood in her front yard staring mean at us. Me and my little sisters Maizell and Hattie sat in the back of our pickup truck. Maizell and I tended to our business, refusing to look at old ugly Big Boy.

But Hattie got to giggling. "She do too look like a monkey!" She yelled, pointing at Big Boy. "Hey, monkey!"

Big Boy stamped over to us and frowned even harder—at me! "You got some nerve, with your pigeon-face self, Raisin! Who you callin' monkey?"

"I didn't call you—"

"Sure do look like a monkey to me!" Hattie whispered real loud behind me.

"Shut up, girl!" I punched my stupid little sister in the shoulder and gave Big Boy a little limp smile, hoping she wouldn't snatch me out of the truck. "Hattie's just actin' crazy."

"She's gonna be crazier if she calls me monkey again, and I'll make you crazy right along with her, see?" Leaning over the side of the truck, Big Boy stuck her face so close to mine that I could see the hairs growing out of her nose.

"Peaches! Beans this mornin'!" Daddy yelled. He started up the truck. We rolled safely away from Big Boy.

"Hat, your mouth is gonna get Raisin killed," said Maizell from behind the peaches and collards baskets. "Big Boy almost made me have to tell her off. Good thing Daddy drove away first."

I could laugh, too. Now. "You got about as much guts to tell somebody off as a handful of mud, and sure not Big Boy."

Fourteen years old, Big Boy was six feet tall, weighed close to two hundred pounds, and could be awful mean when she wanted to be, which was often. She liked to hang around the Gumbo Limbo Soda Fountain and Café. I tried to stay out of her way, and so did everybody else smaller than her who had any sense. Of course, that leaves out Hattie.

I looked up at the sky where two airplanes flew low, trailing banners. One banner read, "Panama Jack Suntan Lotion," and the other one read, "Wet T-shirt Contest Sat. Nite at Hot Rocks." Airplanes flew around with those banners to advertise stuff for folks to do and buy. And did we get folks! They came from all over the world to Gumbo Grove, S.C., "The Number One Family Vacationland." I lived here, too, me and my family and friends. I was eleven years old, and it was *fun* in the summer! Gumbo Grove was supposed to be South Carolina's most famous resort. Which meant that rich folks and try-to-be-rich folks vacationed here, played golf, got lazy in the sun and sand, and swam in the Atlantic Ocean. Folks also came here from all over to work as maids or cooks or salesclerks in the hotels, restaurants, and beachwear shops. That's how we locals made our livings.

They said these were good jobs and that we were lucky to get them, 'cause otherwise we'd have had to work in the tobacco fields making only five dollars a day. Well, I knew people who worked all night cleaning up hotels and condos and then when tobacco harvest-time came, they got out in the fields and worked them, too. I thought they made more than five dollars a day, though. Else why work so hard for so little?

We made part of our living selling vegetables and fruit out of our truck in the neighborhoods. And when we weren't doing that, we sold crabs or did yard work for the people who had those big old homes down by the beach. And Momma and me and sometimes Maizell cleaned up the condos and offices at night. Momma did day work, too, for people, but I didn't. I liked crabbing and selling vegetables the best, but it looked like the vegetables weren't going to make anyone jump up today!

We rattled across the wood bridge spanning the Fifteenth Street drainage ditch and turned onto Cypress Swamp Road. Hattie and Maizell were having a potato fight, throwing the smaller potatoes at each other. It was that slow today. Where were the customers? Not even old Mrs. Alston had bought. It must have been too hot for folks to even come outside to look at what we had to sell.

Just too hot! It got so hot here that the heat hurt your feelings. It was better to be down on the boardwalk with that ocean breeze cooling you off all over. I wished I could go down there right this minute or maybe this afternoon. No, the summer games carnival was going to be held over at the old school this afternoon, and I had told Maizell and Hat that I'd go with them. It wasn't a big deal for me, but it was for them, of course. I wouldn't even have minded going up to Atlantic Beach, S.C. That was an itsy-bitsy resort run by Black folks, with a Black mayor and everything. It was fun to go up there, but I didn't get to go very often because it was quite a few miles away. We went to their Memorial Day Festival, though.

When Daddy crossed onto Strom Thurmond Highway, I knew that he had called it quits and was headed for home. We bumped past the old New Africa No. 1 Missionary Baptist Church standing half up and half down at the side of the road. That's how it looked to me. The back section of the roof was slanted down on the ground, but the front section was still attached to the second story. That had been our family's regular church until our new one was built farther down the highway. I knew all about dates and the history of our church because I loved history. I'd rather find out about history than do anything else. That old church was built back in 1898. It set up on cement blocks, so you could see from one side under it to the other.

Close by the church was the old cemetery,

weedy and scraggly as usual. Hardly anybody was buried in it anymore, not since they started buying at the cemetery over in Deacons Neck ten or fifteen years ago. I'd wondered about the people buried in that old cemetery, but nobody seemed to know anything about them. At least, nobody was talking to me about it.

I asked Daddy once, "Who's buried in there?" And do you know what he said? He said, "Dead people."

In fact, hardly anybody had anything much good to say about anybody else around here. That's how it seemed to me. Unless it was gossip, of course. And when we read about people doing stuff in history class, it was always about White people when it came to Calvary County. Which was okay, but nobody ever mentioned anybody Black. And when I asked Miz Gore, my teacher, how come we never studied about anybody Black who did stuff around here, she said nobody Black around here had ever done anything good worth talking about.

I liked heroes. And I liked to feel good about what people did back in the old days, because it helped me go ahead and feel good about now. But lots of times the kids made fun of me because I talked about heroes like Harriet Tubman and Sojourner Truth. Some of the kids didn't even know who THEY were, and they were real famous.

Bunny and Sin-Sin, my two best friends, said that that was old timey stuff and what about Michael Jackson and Prince? Who were superfine, for true. But that wasn't the same thing.

Just then a woman driving an old rusty Cadillac in the next lane over barreled ahead and spewed strong blue oily smoke all over us. "That car ought to go the junkyard." I coughed. "Wasn't that Miss Effie? About time for her to ask us to do some more work for her, too."

"I don't want to work today," Maizell said.

Well, I knew that. Hattie and Maizell didn't like to do anything but watch TV, roller-skate, dance, and practice cheerleadng jumps. Of course, I liked to do that, too. But I also liked to have a little taste of money. My momma and daddy said you had to work to make money, the honest kind. If people didn't work and didn't want to work, sometimes they sponged off other folks. At least that's what Maizell and Hattie did with me!

Daddy said that after I turned 12 next May he was going to see if I could get a job working at Miz Irene's BarBQue Pit around the corner. And then when I got older I'd maybe get a job at the Burger King or Mc-

Donald's, where I'd be able to wear uniforms. In the meantime, though, I did a lot of odd jobs for Miss Effie.

Miss Effie lived between the old church and the old cemetery, in a little house set back off the road. She was our church secretary and the widow of the Reverend Odell Pfluggins, our pastor from way back when. She liked to play bingo three times a week at Bill's Bingo Barn.

When we got home, I ran over to Momma hanging up clothes in the back yard. She smiled when she saw me, and the star-shaped gold in her right front tooth sparkled. "I bet you all starved, hunh! Go fix some baloney sand-wiches; I got ice tea already made. And Miss Effie wants to know can you all work this afternoon."

When I turned to go to the house, won-dering what Miss Effie wanted us to do, I got pulled to a stop by Momma. Couldn't I hear? she asked. "You ain't growin' down in the gutter; you growin' up in the church," she said.

Ho, boy, that was her favorite saying! She was strict on being polite and respectful. I grinned and said, yes, ma'am, I heard, and that I'd fix lunch and thank you for the message from Miss Effie.

In a few minutes I had lunch ready and gave my sisters their plates. We took them outside to the old tobacco wagon that lay on its side by the okra and collards rows. Zippy and her kittens were already over there, laid back in the shade. When I pinched some meat from my sandwich and threw it on the ground, Toots and Patches pounced on it, but Too Slow just yawned.

"Momma said Miss Effie asked Daddy to go cut weeds at the old cemetery, but he wouldn't do it," I told Hattie and Maizell. "Now Momma says Miss Effie wants us to come help her do something, but she wouldn't tell Momma what it was."

"Like clean up in that ole cemetery? Not me!" Hattie picked up Too Slow and let him sniff her sandwich. "I don't want no plat-eyes on me." She walked away.

Hattie wasn't *really* scared of plat-eyes— some folks called them ghosts—and neither was Maizell. That was just that old laziness coming out. I watched Maizell cram down her sandwich and get to her feet, too. I grabbed her by the arm. "You owe me some money, so don't you be going anywhere."

"I don't owe you so much that I gotta go work in no cemetery! Don't you wanna go to the carnival this afternoon? I do!" Maizell put a whine in her voice like she was going to cry.

"That's for you little kids more'n me. I wanna go to the dance tonight. Plus, we'll be back before then. C'mon."

"I don't wanna clean no cemetery!" She stared at me like she thought I was crazy. She jiggled her arms and legs, working herself up to get madder and madder.

"You don't know that that's what she wants us to do." I wasn't backing off. "C'mon!"

So we went, with Maizell whining and snuffling through her nose on one hand, and with me adding up dimes and quarters in my head on the other. I could hear her carrying on behind me as we rode along on the bicycle path. I speeded my bike up so I wouldn't have to hear.

Miss Effie was waiting. She sat in her lawn chair on the shady side of her house. That way she could watch the mobile homes, vans, campers, and station wagons go by so packed up with people and pillows you thought they ought to explode. She smiled when she saw us. "You think you girls'll be okay working in this hot sun?" she said. "Don't want you to fall out none."

When I said we'd be all right—Maizell said we wouldn't—Miss Effie crossed her legs and cleared her throat. "I reckon you girls can help me with this thing," she said. "You could be so handy with this little place I need cleaned. I got my hoe right here, too. I'll show you how to do."

"What little place?" Maizell asked.

Miss Effie waved her hand in the air. "Right yonder."

"Right yonder where, Miss Effie?"

"Over in the cemetery, Maizell," Miss Effie said real low. "It's nothing hard and won't take but a minute with you big strong girls."

Maizell got to whining again. "Raisin, don't we have to go back and change clothes first?"

"What you got to change clothes for, honey?" Miss Effie asked.

"I—I mean, I got these shorts on," she stammered, "and all those bugs and itchy grass and cockleburrs—"

"She might cut her legs," I said. "Me, too."

Miss Effie sighed and sat back in her chair. "So what can a person do?" She yanked out a red and white flowered handkerchief, slowly pulled off her little gold glasses, and wiped each eye.

Maizell and I looked at each other, knowing that we worked in weeds in our shorts almost all the time, and the bugs and bushes hadn't bothered us much before. I wanted to ask Miss Effie if she was really crying or just scratching her eyeballs. She always liked to make people feel guilty about stuff she wanted them to do that they didn't want to do.

"Why do you have to clean in the cemetery?" I asked instead.

"Because I got something I been trying to get cleaned." She was talking real sad now. "But I can't get nobody to help me. Can't even get nobody to just go in there with me and watch so if I fall out in the sun they could help me get up. By myself, I'm liable to lay out there for days and who would even know?"

"I wanna go to the summer games carnival!" Maizell whined.

"Miss Effie, how far in the cemetery do we have to go to see this spot?" I asked.

"Miss Effie smiled. "It's not too far in; let me show you."

As we walked on the brown sandy trail that ran alongside the chicken wire fence separating the cemetery from Miss Effie's yard, I kept both eyes out for snakes. There are humongous snakes in Calvary County, and they love to lie in the swamps, ditches, weeds, under people's houses, under rocks, wherever they can find a patch of coolness or shade. Like that time over in Deacons Neck when Empie Otis's dad and that rattlesnake went 'round and 'round in their front yard. You're supposed to pour turpentine or sulfur all around your house to keep snakes away. They say turpentine and sulfur lock their jaws up. The turpentine was in the yard, but the snake was, too, and with his mouth wide open. Empie Otis's dad shot that snake. It had sixteen rattles, was six feet long and as thick as my thigh. Empie's daddy hung up the skin in his grocery store for everybody to go "Umph, umph, umph" over.

"I don't wanna go in no cemetery!" Maizell hissed. "And I'm gonna tell Momma if you make me go."

"You girls might as well go back if it's gonna upset you," Miss Effie said. "I'm gonna try even if the good Lord takes me away in the middle of a swing of this hoe."

Well, what can you do when somebody says something like that?

So I dragged Maizell on with me.

Well, we finally got around to the little rickety gate at the back of the cemetery. Two gum trees growing close together served as the cemetery's gateposts, and hooked between them was a piece of chicken wire attached to a couple of boards for a gate. The rest of the fence around the cemetery was connected to trees. You could tell that the trees were young when they put up the fence because now the fence in spots was two or three feet off the ground where the trees had grown.

Using her hoe like a cane, Miss Effie limped to the gate and pulled it open. Gravestones peeked out from clumps of scrub pine trees, tall stringy brown weeds, and what looked like ten years of old bushes and heavy, thorny wild rose and strawberry vines. Tin markers stuck up through bare dirt or lay flattened or bent on the ground. Since I didn't know which spot was a grave and which wasn't, I walked where Miss Effie walked. It was bad luck to step on a grave.

Here and there were faded plastic wreaths on rusty stakes stuck in the sandy soil. I felt like I was supposed to be real scared, but I wasn't.

Miss Effie would stop every so often, lean on her hoe, stare down in the weeds, then sigh long and walk on.

"That's Miz Meriwether's grave there. See how bad it's sunk down? She was one of the top ladies in our usher board and a dear, dear friend of mine. She was the founder of the Calvary County Negro Business and Professional Women's Club—the club that sponsors the Miss Ebony Calvary County Contest? She died before you two was even thought of. She was the one put so much money into keeping the pageant going. She used to own a whole *lot* of land around here and in Cypress Swamp Cove, before it was called that. It's a shame you girls get in that pageant and prance around in your fancy dresses and raise all that money to send to the national but won't even come in here and clean up the founder's grave."

With a grunt Miss Effie struck at the weeds with her hoe until she had cleared them from around a large rock. Faded letters were on the rock, but I couldn't make out what they were. Miss Effie said the rock was Miz Meriwether's headstone. She went on a few more steps, and then she stopped again.

"And this is where Cletus Jackson is buried. Talk about a man could sing! He used to run a little shoeshine stand down on the corner of Hampton Boulevard where the old Guilliard Theater used to be. Shine shoes and sing. That was over fifty years ago, though. He even had his own gospel quartet, and they traveled all around."

Miss Effie talked like she knew everybody buried here. But maybe she did. She must have been ninety years old. Suddenly I remembered Maizell. I stopped and turned around to see what she was doing and almost got run down.

"You better get me out of here," she whispered up against my back. "You the one told me I ain't got no guts. If I have a heart attack out here and die, I'm gonna tell Momma it was all your fault."

The bushes to our right shook.

"Snake!" Maizell shrieked. She flew back through the cemetery. Miss Effie and I watched her go.

"Lord, that child can move," said Miss Effie. Then she said, "Look at her 'snake' there, Raisin."

Sitting in front of the bush by a huge pile of debris, where somebody had piled broken flowerpots, was a small brown rabbit. It didn't seem afraid of us at all. I had to laugh at Maizell and myself, too. I had even been scared.

In a few minutes we came to a huge mound of vines. "What's this, Miss Effie?"

"Baby, that's the tombstone of my husband, and here is his grave," she said. "This ole ramblin' rose grows so fast you can't even keep the tombstone clear." She started to whack at the thicket of thorns and vines covering the tombstone.

"So this is what you want cleaned, hunh."

She nodded and pointed to a spot beside her husband's grave. "And this, too."

"Why?"

" 'Cause I want it to be clean for when my time comes, baby."

I was shocked. "Are you gonna die, Miss Effie?"

"I'll be the first person not to," she said. "Everybody's time comes, baby. 'Course, I don't plan for it to be right now!"

She turned back to the tombstone and with her hoe pulled at the ropes of brown and green. Not knowing what else to do, I pulled at a tiny pine tree with my hands. Tree wouldn't budge. I pulled again. Finally I got down on my knees and fought with it.

"Child, you can go get a hoe out the shed if you want," said Miss Effie, "so's you don't hurt your hands or scrape your legs and knees."

Talk about having a face full of shame! "Yes, ma'am." I jumped up and ran back to the gate quick so she wouldn't see my face showing so much embarrassment from what I said earlier about scratching my legs.

By the time I returned, Miss Effie had uncovered most of the tombstone. It was made of marble, I think, was about four feet tall, and had a wide marble platform around the base. "Sleep in Eternal Peace" was inscribed on the front.

"He was such a fine preacher," she said. "We were born on the same day, same year.

He would have been eighty-eight come August twelfth."

She looked off across the cemetery after she said that. Finally I said, not knowing what else to say, that Reverend Pfluggins must have been a real nice man.

"Bless you," said Miss Effie. "Rev—I always called him Rev—was an angel in church, but one sure-nuff devil at home. I ain't had no more trouble out of him since he died, and I hope to goodness I don't start having trouble when I get here beside him! Do, I'll pick up my casket and move it someplace else!"

She laughed until she had a coughing spell and had to sit down on Reverend Pfluggins's platform. "Old-timers like me still want to be buried out here, honey. We want to be with people we knew. You got all kinds of kinfolk out here, too. Bet you didn't know that. Two great-uncles from your mother's side, your great-great-grandparents on both sides, and Lord knows how many great-aunts and cousins."

"Momma never said anything about us having kin out here," I said. "We always go over to the cemetery at Deacons Neck on Memorial Day to clean the graves. Guess it's too hard to find graves out here. Or maybe the folks died too long ago to worry about."

Miss Effie puffed up like an angry old blowfish. "Your ancestors are never too old to honor, Miss Lady. If it hadn't been for them you wouldn't be here now, and neither would nobody else."

She lifted the hoe a couple times and whacked the blade in the dirt and weeds. "I know about where almost everybody's buried here except for the real early people. When I say early, I mean the ones barely buried this side of freedom. Some folks buried in here were still slaves even after the freedom came. Nobody told them any different. So they just kept slavin' away till they died, and the master had them brought over here. That's what I always heard."

Girl, talk about somebody pricking up her ears! Was this history? Right under my nose all these years? Why hadn't Momma or Daddy told me about our folks being buried here, too? Maybe that was why I had so many holes in the family tree that Hattie and Maizell and I were trying to complete. Maybe they weren't anybody special. But I sure wanted to know more about them!

When Miss Effie saw that I was interested,

she told me that prominent people were buried there, too. "But I guess they ain't prominent anymore, 'cause the ones who thought of them that way's dead, too. I could tell you one big name that would shake this town upside down if folks knew he was buried out here and who he really was."

daddy soon's as ole Mr. Vereen, the master, found out he was gone. Zeke was one of his best slaves. He was a blacksmith. Without Zeke, ole Mr. Vereen couldn't shoe his horses or keep his plows sharp, and so on. They looked for Zeke, but he was gone. Ole Mr. Vereen asked Gussie all kinds of questions. I mean, *all* kinds. But she wouldn't tell him a thing about her daddy. Wouldn't even say his name. She was waiting and praying on January. But think how that child must have suffered something awful all alone like that!

"When the year come to a close, she had to been fit to bust. Daddy said he heard that all she ever did talk about was going to Singleton's Shrimp place. Miz Vereen and her daughter Hazel May got wind of what Gussie was saying about Singleton's. It didn't take them long to put two and two together. Ole Mr. Vereen, his ole wife, and Hazel May set a trap for Gussie Ann and her daddy. They said Mr. Singleton at the dock needed somebody for a couple of months to get his boats and shop readied for the next season, and did Gussie know any house girls want to go?

"Poor little Gussie worked in the fields. She wasn't a house girl. But she begged and begged and did extra in the fields to make them see what a good worker she could be for

Mr. Singleton, and that she could work as hard, or harder, than any house girl could.

"They said yes, she could go.

"The overseer took Gussie. Well, he rode his horse; she walked. Walked! All the way to Georgetown from Lime Hill, fifteen, twenty miles!

"Singleton didn't seem to know anything about Vereen's plot to get her daddy. But he was mean, too, or just didn't care she was so young. He put her to work as soon as she got there, after walking all those miles!

"Slave kids worked harder back then than grown folks do in the fields today! They didn't have any kind of machinery to help them, either, you understand? Gussie had those cold ropes and nets to fix and haul around? She had to work straight on the water, too? Ole cold raw wind blowing in off that water? Daddy said he heard her fingers froze two or three times that winter.

"Singleton couldn't find a bit of fault with her work. She could clean and shell shrimp and clam and oyster just as good as anybody, and cook them all, too. She learned how to split flounder and spots and croaker fish and how to bleed bluefish so the meat wouldn't get mushy when it was cooked. She even learned how to hold a jellyfish in the palm of her hand

and not get stung. And of course she knew how to do the hard stuff like repair the ropes and nets and how to scrub.

"Ten years old. Orphan. Scrubbing down boats in that ole cold raw wind.

"The year finally finished, and the new one came in. The third Saturday arrived. Gussie probably got up extra early that morning and probably tried to get all her work done quick, excited about her daddy coming, not knowing exactly when.

"But he didn't show up. He didn't show up the next day. Or the next week or the next month. Some say he might have come for her before that time and missed her. Nobody knows for sure but that he didn't get her. Isn't that a pitiful thing? My daddy said he heard she got so she would hardly eat a thing. Which of course made her weak. She still had all that work to do. And she did it, best she could. But they say she cried so hard after her pa in that winter cold that her right eye froze over.

"One morning she didn't come out of the shed where they had her staying. Singleton called and called for her. Finally he went in the shed and found her dead on her little pallet. She had grieved herself to death.

"Ole Miz Vereen had them bury her over here so they wouldn't have to bring her all the way back to the Vereens' slave cemetery. That's the way the story went. But I think ole Vereen and his wife were ashamed about how they let that child be treated so bad. I think they couldn't bear to have her grave too close to them.

"I heard tell that this little Gussie had an aunt living over on the Vereen farm and that this aunt used to come over here and tend Gussie's grave up until around 1900. This aunt had some children who went all whichaways after they got grown, but some of them settled around Gumbo Grove. Yeah! Gussie got kin right here! And not a one of them come out here to tend her grave.

"One of the kin is that big gal named Pansey Burroughs, the one they call Big Boy? Though she probably don't know about Gussie. The one who does know, though, is Big Boy's grandmother, that Aussie Skipper. She thinks her ancestors are so high and mighty and never been slaves. She knows better. She's kin to Gussie, too, of course."

Gussie Ann Vereen! Miz Skipper! Big Boy! I was about to bust with questions, but before I could get started, Miss Effie got going again.

"There's a group of folks right in our own church who think this old cemetery ought to be dug up and moved to the one in Deacons Neck, and that the old church ought to be torn down. Some of them who think they know everything say the church and the cemetery are eyesores. And you know who's leading the charge?"

Miss Effie beetled her eyebrows at me fiercely. "Aussie Skipper! She's trying her best to get the church to sell this land to one or another of her ole so-called politician friends. That'll give her pull and make her think she's even more uppity-up. See, this is prime land and right on the highway, Raisin. Many a man's wanted to buy, but none ever has got past me to do it! I'm church secretary!"

Miss Effie waved her hand in the air like she was shaking hands with the Lord. She looked like she was in church and was full of the spirit. "But they'll never get it done! All this is church property—the cemetery, the church, and this very house. They can't tear nothing down because the records say they got to stand until the church body votes to change it. And I swear I'm not about to let them change it because I got the records, and I'm not giving them up to her!"

"To who, Miss Effie?"

"You're not listening, Raisin. To Miss Aussie!" Miz Skipper wanted to be church secretary and change everything around, said Miss Effie, because then she would have more power than even the pastor. "Miz Skipper and me been going around on this for years and years, with Miz Skipper trying to get the property sold and propagandizing that I was too old to be church secretary."

As I listened, I began to get worried. Moving the graves from the cemetery and tearing down the church would take away a part of our own history! Just when I was starting to hope that maybe we finally had some! What kind of sense did that make?

"She'll sell it over my dead body!" She stopped suddenly. "And, honey," she said calmly, "I don't plan to die real soon."

"Oh, good." I sighed with relief. So much talk about death made me worried.

"And don't pay attention about me cleaning off my plot. I'm just being practical."

I remembered that Momma and Daddy didn't have much good to say about the cemetery and the old church, either. I guess they were on Miss Aussie's side, too. But if everybody got together and voted against Miss Effie, she wouldn't have much say about what happened. And I wouldn't have any history or heroes, if there actually were any, from my own hometown. And that made me feel bad.

"But we gotta try, Miss Effie! I'll help you," I found myself saying. "They're gonna have to run me off, too."

I skidded to a stop. Could Gussie be a hero? And maybe Miz Meriwether, too! Even if they were from right here? Seem like they could! I wasn't sure, though. I thought I'd see what Momma had to say about them.

As soon as I got home, Momma asked me how it went. "Well, we cleaned in the cemetery. Talk about full of history! Miss Effie told me about this girl named Gussie Ann buried in it." I told her the story.

Momma just said, "Hmmmm."

"And I'm gonna keep a journal and write down every word Miss Effie says and then I'll know everything about everybody."

She looked sharp at me and then sa
"Humph."

I got impatient. "Humph? What does *humph*
mean?"

"That ole woman is good for spreading
gossip is what it means. Raisin, honey, that
cemetery over there is so depressing. Lots of
those stories ain't pretty to hear. I thought
they were going to dig up those graves and
tear down that church. I thought Miz Skipper
and them had got it settled. Guess not."

Then, smiling at me, she thumped me
lightly on the shoulder with her fist. "And my
baby thought she found some history and she's
raring to go! Miss Professor History Teacher."

I grinned, proud that she remembered
how much I wanted to be a history teacher. I
hoped she wouldn't say I couldn't keep a
journal.

What Momma said was that I shouldn't
pay half a handful of attention to what Miss
Effie said. "She's so up in age, you know. She's
liable to get everything mixed up and tell it to
you mixed up, too. People get awful sensitive
about the things that go on in their families.
I'd hate for folks to get riled up over something
you wrote wrong from what she told you
wrong."

...ted out where Miz Meriwether too."

...ma looked puzzled. "Who's that?"

...he lady who founded our pageant, don't remember?"

"Of course, of course." She didn't look like she remembered, though. "Miss Effie talks too daggone much. She'll have you and her and me, too, run out of town. You be careful, hear?"

"I'll be careful." Whew. At least she didn't say that I couldn't keep a journal, right?

Maizell and Hattie were in the kitchen jabbering about what happened at the carnival.

"Momma said I didn't have to work in no cemetery if I didn't want to," Maizell said to me. I shrugged, went out to the okra patch and watered the plants until it was time to eat supper.

Later the telephone rang. It was Bunny Walterboro saying I just *had* to go with her to get a Coke at the Gumbo Limbo. I said okay and told Momma, then went outside in the hot, wet, briny evening air. It must have been close to nine o'clock and still so hot I got sweaty all over again. In the distance I could hear a radio playing some fast music. Made me want to dance.

I saw Bunny waiting for me under the

streetlight by Miz Irene's BarBQue Pit. She saw me. "Big Boy says she's gonna beat you up!" she hollered. "She's waiting at the Gumbo Limbo."

Naturally I stopped walking fast. "She's lyin'," I hollered back.

"She say she tired of your mouth! I told her she better quit talking about my friend 'cause you don't take no mess. That's when she said she was gonna beat—"

"Thanks, Bunny." We were face to face now. "Big Boy's already been in my face over something Hattie said, and now here you go!"

Bunny giggled, then doubled over, laughing hard.

"What's so daggone funny?" I was getting mad.

"You gotta gimme five on that one." She flipped out her hand for me to slap her palm. "I ain't even seen Big Boy today! God, you shoulda seen your face! You looked like you were gonna cry!"

I was so relieved that I went ahead and slapped her hand. Better Bunny be getting me than Big Boy!

"Ain't you goin' to the disco? I been waitin' and waitin' for you to call. I thought maybe you got grounded or something. Your momma likes to ground you all the time. Can you go?"

"Oh, wow, I forgot!" I started to tell her about the cemetery, but she cut in.

"Girl, we missin' everything. They jammin' at the school yard. Can't you hear that music? Tashia said the whole yard is packed. Oh, listen! They just put on Prince! Come on!"

I forgot about the Coke.

When we got to the school yard, we saw folks bobbing hard in time to the music. Under a floodlight in the middle of the kids was Crackers De Veux, the DJ, rocking back. On the basketball court nearby guys had enough light to play a hard, fast, smooth game of Twenty-One.

I could smell orange soda, hot dogs, cigarette smoke, and Gloria Vanderbilt perfume everywhere. It was a grown crowd, sixteen- and seventeen-year-olds, though I saw a few kids my age. I started a quick step right there all by myself, but Bunny pulled at me. She wanted to talk to Crackers, and I had to go with her. Crackers was okay, I guess, but he was seventeen years old and way too old for me. Not too old for Bunny, though. She was thirteen and said she was a woman. She looked about sixteen and grown. I looked eleven and average—average height, dark brown, jerry curl, good teeth, and a dimple.

We pushed through the dancers until we

got over to the table. Bunny big-eyed and dimpled him hard. Crackers dimpled back at her. Leaning toward his mike, he said in his deep, slow voice, "Bunny sweets, this song's for you."

Bunny's face lit up like a sparkler on the Fourth of July. When the song was over, Bunny was still wired up. But suddenly she frowned. "Look out, here comes trouble."

Sneering, feet spread wide, elbowing folks out of the way, Big Boy clumped up to Bunny with her hands on her hips. "You out kinda late, aren't ya?" she sniffed at Bunny. "Ain't them babies of your momma calling you, Miss Rabbit? Better hip-hop back to your raggedy house and feed all them brats."

"Big Boy," somebody behind us said, "shovel up your mouth."

"Who said that?" Big Boy glared around her, and then she saw me.

"C'mon, girl," I whispered frantically to Bunny, "let's split!"

"And you here, too, Miss Pigeon Face," Big Boy said to me. "Lemme hear you talk big now that you don't have no raggedy truck to hide in!"

I kept my mouth shut and stared back at her like I wasn't scared. Which is a lie, because I was!

The music ended and everything got quiet. Big Boy looked around to make sure she had an audience. She looked me up and down like she was trying to figure out where she would bite me first. Duck that first blow and then tromp her on the foot good, I stuttered to myself, trying to stare back at her just as hard. Squat down quick to duck the next blow, shoot up, and butt her chin hard with your head and then *run*!

Crackers's voice rolled out over the speaker. "You messin' up my disco, Big Boy. Leave them little sisters alone."

Whew!

Big Boy stared evilly at us, but she didn't dare go against Crackers. He was in charge. So she turned up one nostril at me and switched away.

"Now let's jam," Crackers said.

Tell the truth, I was ready to jam on home! But wasn't it exciting! Near bloodshed! Who-fought-who gossip was hot! Maybe everybody would talk about Bunny and me and Big Boy almost having bloodshed.

That puffed me up with vanity until my brain told me to please think on what my folks would do if they ever found out. Found out? Sweet Jesus. Suddenly I remembered. I hadn't said anything to Momma about going to any disco. Time to go!

But when I turned to tap Bunny on the shoulder, I caught Crackers smiling at me. He winked at me, which flattered me so much that I stayed by his table listening a few more minutes. "I gotta go buy that Coke," I finally told Bunny, "and get home before I get in any more trouble."

"Don't you like Mellow Yellow? That tastes better."

"No, I need Coke!"

Two or three kids who heard me stared at me funny. I bet they thought I meant dope! Dumb, dumb, dumb! I knew it was time to go for real then, and I did, quick!

I hotfooted over to Mr. Alston's carport to his soda machine, popped in two quarters. Praise the Lord, he had Coca-Cola.

When I slunk into our yard, I saw Daddy, but he was asleep and I was glad. That way he couldn't ask me any hard-to-answer questions, like how come it took you two hours to get a can of pop?

Daddy snored once so deep I giggled. He liked to sleep out on the front porch couch in the summer when the heat got bad. He slept all twisted up on the couch like this: flat on his back on the couch, but with his feet on the floor.

Momma wouldn't sleep outside for nobody. She said when she was a girl she was sleeping in this big tent at Sunday School camp one time? She said she saw a big old water moccasin slide down the tent pole into the room! She said she woke everybody up by tearing a hole in the side of the tent, trying to get out. From then on she slept indoors in a place where there were real doors tight against real floors that didn't have any holes. She said if God had wanted her to sleep outside, He would have brought her into the world as a bear.

I went into the dark living room.

"Is that you?" Momma asked from the bedroom.

"Yes, ma'am." I held my breath. But she didn't say anything else. I could hear the television in our room. But I didn't feel like gossiping with Hattie and Maizell. I wanted to think about the dance tonight—and my notes.

Hurrying to the kitchen, I fixed myself a sandwich and, after plunking some ice cubes into a glass, went into the living room. I pulled my notes from my shorts pocket, turned on the lamp, and lay down on the couch to read.

Next thing I knew, Momma was shaking

my shoulder and telling me to get up and get ready for church. Sunday morning already.

To me, our new New Africa No. 1 Missionary Baptist Church was the prettiest church in the whole county. Bright white stucco on the outside, with a bell and blue-tinted glass in the steeple. At night, with the steeple lit, the church looked like a castle. Inside was smooth pinewood paneling throughout the sanctuary. High rafters and stained-glass windows. On the wall behind the pulpit was this huge, fuzzy, rainbow-colored wall hanging of the Last Supper, the biggest I had ever seen, with a Black Jesus.

And we had microphones all over the place. Gospel groups liked to sing at our church and cut records. We had the best P.A. system in town. There were mikes on stands by each collection table, one by the podium, three in the pulpit, and one over each choir box. Anyone who was nervous about being in the Christmas play or the church pageant didn't have to walk far on shaky legs to get to a microphone here! 'Course, *my* legs didn't shake, because I liked to be on the program, and I *loved* to be in pageants. Like Miss Ebony!

Which was what I thought about while I sat in church only half listening to Reverend Walker. What was I going to do for a talent this year? Beside me were Bunny and her brother and sisters and my sisters, and my parents. Candy, Bunny's three-year-old sister, was sick with a head cold, which made her grouchy-bad! Bunny rocked her on her lap, but it didn't do any good.

"That ole germ's just doin' a job on this baby, ain't it?" she whispered to Candy, who kept up a low-pitched whine. Puddin, Candy's twin sister, was asleep against Bunny's other arm. "I oughta left you home to sleep."

"Yeah, but Momma woulda got mad if Candy and Puddin got too loud and woke her up," said their brother Pooch, who always heard everything. He was in third grade and still couldn't read or write, no matter how much we tried to help him. He was good in kick soccer, though.

Just about the time Reverend Walker would have told us to stand for the benediction, Miss Effie tiptoed over to Deacon Moultrie and whispered something in his ear. Deacon Moultrie leaned back and whispered something to Reverend Walker.

"I'm so sorry, Miz Pfluggins, for slighting you," Reverend Walker said. "Miz Pfluggins will now make her two special announcements."

Straightening her skirt, Miss Effie came to

the microphone by the collection table and thanked Reverend Walker for calling on her. "First, I want you all to remember the Miss Ebony Pageant that the Calvary County Negro Business and Professional Women will hold. We certainly look to you individuals and businesses for financial support. So when the girls come by asking you to buy an ad, please say yes. And please give them the money right then."

She talked like that for a while, sounding as if she was wound up tight enough to hang out with an eight-day clock. "And now I think the church at this time ought to give a special young lady recognition for a most important task that lies ahead." She stopped again, to let that sink in. "She's a hard little worker, and she's just going to be so handy with helping me write the history of the New Africa Number One Missionary Baptist Church cemetery. Raisin Stackhouse, honey, will you please stand up and come to the front?"

Shocked, I jumped up and couldn't help but feel embarrassed by the big buildup she gave me. For what? I hadn't done anything yet. I started to move past Momma to go up to the front when I glanced around at the people sitting next to us. I noticed Mr. Manigault was frowned up, and so was his wife.

When Momma slid out her feet so that I'd have to step over them to get past, I stayed where I was and just turned around to face the congregation. Miz Aussie Skipper, who sat two pews behind, had the strangest expression on her face. So did Mr. Alston and Miz Rapture and some other folks. When they saw me look at them, they smiled, but around those funny expressions.

Maybe Miss Effie shouldn't have told the church what we planned to do. Some of those folks who didn't like the cemetery—the ones looking funny, maybe?—might make us stop before we even got going good. When Momma pulled at my dress, I sat down. She smiled a little at me, and Daddy nodded, but he had that same look, too.

Pooch leaned over, whispering. "You gonna dig up bones in that ole cemetery, and them bones are gonna come after you."

"Behave, you're in church," Bunny told him. "You ain't supposed to talk about the dead like that."

"See, I told you that's where she was," Maizell said to Bunny, "in the cemetery. I coulda helped her, but I didn't want to."

Big Head—Jeff Thomas, who sat in the next pew—turned around and grinned at me. He was tall, skinny, and was thirteen years old.

He thought he was so smart because he used to live in Columbia, our state capital. He bragged so much about Columbia that everyone calls him Big Head. He used to have a jerry-curl hairstyle, but shaved his head and now has a Carl Lewis cut. We still call him Big Head.

Tell the truth, I thought he was kinda cute. So I blinked my eyes wide at him and tried not to look too proud with myself.

Church got out, but it wasn't over. Miss Aussie hurried toward me. "Raisin, aren't you a busy little girl?" she said.

Just to be on the safe side, I said thank you real polite. But you know, if glue could talk, it would sound just like Miss Aussie—sticky! She acted sticky, too, like she was always trying to catch you in a trap.

"How you doing this morning, Miz Skipper?" Daddy said. "He preached a nice sermon, didn't he?"

"Praise the Lord, he sure enough did. And like he said, the devil's work is all around us, but it's up to us to nip that devilishness in the bud," she answered. Then she rolled her eyes around and fixated on me. "Isn't it?"

Reverend Walker and Miss Effie came over, too. "So you're going to do some work in the cemetery?" Reverend Walker said to me. "Isn't that wonderful!"

"Yes, sir," I said, glad that he was pleased. Reverend Walker taught history at Gumbo Grove Middle School and was historian of the Missionary Baptist Convention in our district.

"But why," said Miss Aussie, "don't we take this up with the burying league or the deacons first and see can we get this history straight before anyone goes spreading rumors and tales?"

"Won't be rumors or tales," Miss Effie snapped, giving Miss Aussie a strong eyeballing. "This is coming from the church records and me! I've been church secretary forty-six years and not a word in the records has been found unstraight yet, has it?"

There was this pause where nobody said anything.

Miss Aussie pasted on one of her sticky smiles. "Well, we've got to be strict what all we're going to say when we go poking around in other folks' business, don't we, Reverend Walker?"

Everybody turned to Reverend Walker, who had turned his back to us to talk to Miz Florence Gooddell. Reverend Walker stared at Miss Aussie blankly. Then he smiled. "Talking about cemeteries brings back that all-night revival I had near a cemetery over in Pickens County."

Miss Effie pulled me off to one side. "I'll have a big yellow pound cake waiting for you if you come sit a spell with me this afternoon," she whispered.

"Oh, thanks, I was gonna ask if I could come," I whispered back. We grinned at each other, and then I hurried away from everybody, especially Miss Aussie.

As I went out the door, Big Head reached out and hit me on the elbow. "If you wanna see famous cemeteries, you oughta go to Columbia. It's got cemeteries with Civil War heroes and congressmen."

"I don't want to go to Columbia," I said, and asked the Lord to pardon me.

"You oughta see the ones in Washington, D.C., too," he went on. "I like Washington. I been there lots of times."

"I don't wanna see Washington, either, Big Head," I said, telling another one. Lord knew how much I wanted to get out and see the world. I'd hardly even stepped one toe out the county, not even to Columbia.

Hattie, Maizell, Bunny, Sin-Sin, and the rest of the kids standing under the pine tree hollered at me to come over. I knew they were going to work me over about ghosts.

"Plat-eye ghost's gonna get you, Raisin," said Sin-Sin. "Plat-eye ghost's gonna come in your house, slide under your door into your room, hop on your back, and ride you all night long, just like you was an ole mule. You be thinking you're having the horriblest dream, but it'll be that ole plat-eye riding you."

"I ain't scared of nobody's plat-eye," I said. I crossed my toes inside my shoes, just in case. "And I bet you never even seen one, neither."

Ursula hollered that her daddy had. "And it had big red eyes. Daddy saw it on Cypress Swamp Road just about night when he was a little boy. He say he and some other guys were walking back from fishing in the creek—the part that's up around Cypress Swamp Cove where those condos are now. Him and his Uncle Toe and them.

"He had left his knife back at the creek where they'd been fishing? He decided to go back to get it. The others went on. He had a bucket half full of spots, too. But Daddy say he went back through the swamp grass along the edge of the creek and found his knife. It was moonlight out, see, so he didn't have no problem.

"On the way back he kept thinking something was following him, but when he would look around, he wouldn't see a thing. Just as he got onto the bridge over the creek he felt his back start to get real hot right under his shoulderblades? He said it was like two pins were being burned into his back. He said when he jumped to one side, he looked back and saw two huge round eyes red as blood with steam rising from them hanging in the air not two feet behind him. He started walking backwards from those eyes, trying not to look into them, because a plat-eye can suck your breath out if it can catch your eyes and hypnotize you? Still holding on to his knife in one hand and the bucket in the other, he hit across that bridge and didn't stop until he caught up with Toe and them.

"But you know what? All the fish in his bucket was gone. Daddy said that plat-eye got 'em."

"You a lie and a grunt," said Pooch. "You told me your daddy grew up in North Carolina."

"I seen a plat-eye," said Sin-Sin, "and it wasn't nothin' like that, girl."

"That might have been the spirit of Miz Meriwether or Gussie Ann," I said.

"Who's that?" Hattie wanted to know.

"Miz Meriwether was the founder of the Miss Ebony Pageant, and she owned a bunch of land around where Ursula's daddy said he was. And Gussie—"

"Didn't nobody Black ever own a bunch

of land or a bunch of anything around here."
Hattie was scornful. "People be lucky if they
got a house, let alone any land. These ole
cheap people?"

"But Miss Effie said—"

"One time I hear Miss Aussie tell Reverend
Walker that Miss Effie was losing her marbles,"
Ursula said. "She lost another one when she
told you that. You're starting to sound crazy,
too!"

Everybody laughed at me and went, "Shuh."

Fussing about Miz Meriwether and her
land, we all walked back to our folks, who were
standing in the parking lot. My face was hot.
What Miss Effie had said to me had made
sense, but it sure didn't seem to go over very
well with anybody else. Maybe they knew something I didn't. Maybe—maybe I wanted to
make folks into heroes too quick, you know?
The way these ones here were acting today,
they sure didn't *act* like heroes. But I also
figured that if Miss Effie told me something
crazy, I'd know it.

And take my soul to Jesus if I didn't,
because the rest of me, for sure, would be in
some sure nuff trouble.

Later at dinner Hattie said I was weird.
"Well, you are," she said with her mouth full
of okra. "And Daddy, ain't she gonna get

grabbed by a plat-eye, fooling around in that graveyard?"

"She's more likely gonna get grabbed by Miss Aussie and Deacon Rapture," Daddy said. "You mind, Raisin, what Miss Effie says. She don't row with both oars! I remember one time she had us believing that Easter fell on the sixteenth of March. Everybody took her word for it 'cause she was church secretary, see? We got ready for the Easter program, and we got our programs printed up. You know what? She'd give us the wrong blamed date! Already sent the announcement to the papers and the radios and everything! Made the church look like a fool!"

"Since then I've been double-checking every date she mentions," Momma added. "She can turn words into rubber bands, way she twists them up stometimes. I don't know about you writing all this stuff down."

"Can't you look at what I write after she tells me, and let me know what's right and what's wrong?"

"How we gonna know what is and what isn't when she gets to talking about things that happened way back when?" Momma asked. "I can't see that all that stuff's gonna be in the record books. She's not supposed to be keeping a diary. Those are church record books."

"Well, can I ask Reverend Walker to read what I write, too?"

"Child don't give up, does she?" Daddy said to Momma.

They finally said it was okay for me to go get "research" at Miss Effie's—*this* time. After that, they'd see.

As soon as dinner was over, I flew around clearing off the table and taking the food into the kitchen, where Momma was. "I remember the time Miss Effie wrote a piece for the newspaper," she said, "and she had people's names spelled wrong left and right. She had Reverend Roses pastoring at the wrong church. And you should have heard the ruckus when our usher board hosted forty usher boards in our district! She had written out a greeting on a big banner that our ladies were supposed to carry into the church at the start of the program? But wouldn't nobody carry that devilish thing 'cause she had *Jubilee* spelled with two *o*'s instead of a *u*. Talk about us being hot!"

"Well, everybody makes mistakes," I said real low.

Before I left for Miss Effie's, I packed my writing equipment into my duffel bag: tape recorder, fresh double-A batteries, new notebook, three fine-point pens, cassette tapes—

everything there! I believed in having good backup, see. I threw my duffel bag on my back, hopped on my bike, and was off.

And as I pedaled hard past the grove of palmetto trees where I sometimes stopped to rest, I told myself and told myself, "Remember what they warned you on." I also couldn't wait to get there.

Under her live oak tree Miss Effie stood waiting. "Hey, baby. You're a mighty good sight for sore eyes. Thought you might not get here." All her wrinkles curled up into a big smile. "Have a piece of this pound cake and some tea."

She let me eat for a while, then told me to get out my writing works. I wanted to ask her about all those mistakes everybody said she made, but I wasn't sure how to do it. So I didn't. In fact, I felt kind of funny all of a sudden, like maybe she shouldn't tell me anything else. Maybe she *was* crazy.

"Did anybody mention the name Sarvis Exile to you?" Miss Effie asked me. "No? I'm not surprised. People don't like to talk about what happened to him."

"What happened to him?"

"That's what I'm about to tell you. Sarvis Exile owned a bunch of that beach right there on the ocean where you all crave to go. Do you remember that I said you had people buried in this cemetery? He was one of them."

My mouth fell open. Quickly I set down my plate and turned on my tape recorder, eager to find out who this mysterious relative was.

Sarvis Exile
(born 1892, died October 17, 1952)

Told to Me by
Miss Effie Pfluggins

June 15

"Your great-uncle Sarvis Exile was a fisherman, and right respectable. People came from everywhere in the county to buy his fish—spots, sea bass, flounder bigger than you'll ever see now, blue crabs, stone crabs, shark meat—anything moving in the ocean one day was liable to end up swimming in his nets the next. He lived in a little-bitty shack right on the beach, and that's where he sold his fish.

"Sarvis Exile once owned a whole mile of Gumbo Grove's most expensive waterfront property. In fact, the Pavilion headquarters sits where Sarvis's house used to be. And where all those amusement rides, wax museums and bingo shows and such, the boardwalk, are? That all used to be his land. Folks today act like that boardwalk is the prettiest thing since the Lord created Florida. But right along in the old days it was prettier 'cause it had sand dunes and clean sand, clear blue water and sunrises with no planes and banners crisscrossing everywhere.

"And it 'most all belonged to us then. We don't so much as own an inch of it now.

"Sarvis built his little house right out behind the tide line on a sand dune and was as happy as a clam living down there.

"We all tried to own land. We had owned all that land from the ocean at Sarvis's beach clear across Hampton Boulevard and on over to Cypress Swamp Road. Back then it was mostly scrub pine, swamp rats, and dirt roads. Didn't nobody but us see much good in it. And the good we saw wasn't much.

"A thousand dollars was a lot of money back in the 1920s and 1930s for us, Raisin.

Most of us was some awfully poor Black people back in them days. So it was triple hard for us to get even a little bit more, you know?

"Back then the only folks here were scrub farmers living on the Deacons Neck side of the Big Sing River. They had a hard enough time making a living out of dirt, let alone try to make it out of sand. Didn't care one penny about the beach. So the few of us who could buy did, and bought cheap. We didn't know what we really had.

"Your uncle Sarvis did, though.

" 'Cause things changed. Farmers' sons grew up, went yonder to New York, got smart, came back, and wanted that sand. So we sold cheap, too. Bought cheap and sold cheap. Didn't know any better.

"This is how it came to be for your uncle Sarvis. After World War Two, people began to want more vacation space. They were tired of going to Florida. They'd be coming from New Jersey and New York and Vermont and them way north cold places, toward Florida, and they'd get here and like it. Then they'd build. And back and forth and so on until everybody up north, it seemed, had heard of Gumbo Grove and wanted to come down here. And they did, and they took over. Buy and build, buy and build.

"But your uncle Sarvis bought, too.

"Now us. We started to come in from the country outlying Gumbo Grove, from Horseshoe Swamp, Ten Lost Swamp, King's Island, Turner's Isle, up and down the coast. Oh, we'd clean the hotels and motels, wash clothes, cook, curl and crimp, lug and lift. Making pennies and dimes. Don't laugh! That was good money for folks who didn't have any.

"Well, these motels and hotels just popped up along the beach—except where Sarvis still owned his beachfront property. He still had his little house on it, too. Thing looked almost like it was laughing at those big motels all around it. Like it had its own little empire in the middle of that mile. Those White folks didn't like him being there.

"You know, we used to could walk up and down the beach everywhere for miles and miles if we wanted to—us Colored—but after those hotels came along, the White folks wouldn't let us put so much as a toe on their beach. So when we wanted to go to the beach, the only part we could walk on was Sarvis's part. And the only part of the ocean that we could swim or wade in was the part directly in front of Sarvis's beach.

"That was called segregation. You mustn't ever forget that word. Gumbo Grove was just as segregated a place as you could ever imagine, which you can't, since you never lived under it where you could see it plain. But try to picture this: just because you're Black you can't go into the Pavilion down on that boulevard to play them video games. Can't nobody Black rent a room in not a one of the fancy hotels, let alone hold a conference in one, or have a big parade down Ocean Boulevard.

"Just imagine that the only way you'd be hanging out at the Pavilion was if you had a broom or a mop in your hand. That's how it was for us back in the days just before Gumbo Grove started to grow.

"And another thing. We couldn't go into no dressing room and try on any clothes. You had to buy first and hope it fit, second. You couldn't take them back, either. Same thing for shoes. Many a girl I know messed up her feet over a pair of too-small black patent-leather pumps. That's how come so many of us got bad feet now. Couldn't try them on!

"Couldn't eat at any lunch counters or restaurants, even though we were the ones did the cooking most of the time. Sometimes they'd let you buy something to eat, though, if you went to the kitchen and ordered it, and ate it outside. That was the real 'to go'! Once in a while there might be a little room in the back where the Colored could eat. Sometimes be more crowded in the back than in the rest of the whole restaurant. But we'd be having some fun! No liquor, of course.

"If you were downtown and had to go to the bathroom or get a drink of water, you had to use the toilet or the water fountain set aside just for us. But that wasn't an advantage, honey. Half the time the fountains didn't work and the other half they were so filthy you couldn't get to them. And if you were in a hurry and someone was in the Colored toilet, you couldn't go into the White one. No, Lord! You could get arrested!

"Colored women couldn't wear shorts or even pedal pushers downtown. But, being a preacher's wife, wearing pedal pushers and shorts was a sin to me anyway, so that part didn't bother me.

"Well, your uncle Sarvis hung on to that beach and hung on to that beach. But the big motel and hotel owners began buying us poor little folks out, White and Black. One or two of us were smart and made a few dollars when we sold; most of us weren't and of course didn't.

"The ones that didn't? The buyers would get them to put their X on a piece of paper.

People who couldn't read or write signed their names with X.

"So, he paid you by rolling a hundred dollar bill around a roll of newspaper cut to the same size. He'd give that roll to them poor people. Since they couldn't read, they wouldn't know what they signed. Since they were most scared of the White people and the few powerful Colored, they didn't dare say no to whatever amount of money they got. Plus, all they could see was that hundred dollar bill. Probably looked like a thousand dollars to them. When they found out different, they just gave up. They threw up their hands and said let it go.

"We didn't have lawyers ready to help us back then like we do now. There wasn't a single Negro lawyer in this county until the 1970s, and that's a fact. You had to go over to some other county to find one. And sometimes they'd treat you dirty, too, and trick you out of your property. People did it to each other all over, honey, Black and White. They sure Lord did it to us here.

"After the big powerful folks got the beach, except for Sarvis's, they went after the folks who had most valuable land second-closest to the ocean. Now, a couple of these particular folks were much better off than the folks living right on the beach. You couldn't do much with land that's just sand and shells if you were poor. But this second-closest land was different, so you got a few folks with a bit more money and more sense. Like Miz Meriwether.

"Miz Alfronia DeCosta Meriwether! She owned all that ground above the mall, from where the civic center and the utility company sit to about over to where the Hampton Boulevard Office Complex is. Miz Meriwether had come over from Greenville thirty-some years earlier and was a companion sitter. That means she sat with old rich folks who would vacation down here trying to get well. They usually didn't. Some of them left her money in their wills. She used it to buy land. But then she had to get greedy and crooked, in her own way, too.

"During slavery times we couldn't own anything, remember. After the freedom came, some of us bought land, but sometimes we didn't get a deed to prove it. Not knowing we were supposed to was one part of it, and getting cheated was the other. And some of us stayed right on at the same place where we'd been slaves, just kept staying there, and old master wouldn't say nothing.

"We sharecropped for him, and he fed and sheltered us right along. Most of us stayed in debt to him, too. He'd promise that the land was ours forever because we'd been so faithful, and then he'd turn around and die. We thought the land was ours. His children would come along and tell us to pay rent or move off. We'd say the land was ours. They'd ask for the deed. We wouldn't have one. But *they* would.

"Miz Meriwether got ten or fifteen good parcels of land, buying it out from under folks who thought they had a deed. The people had to pay rent to her or move.

"Lots of Colored around here didn't like her because of her being so mean like that, but they were more afraid of her power. Plus she did so much other good for the community.

"Miz Aussie Skipper buys land like that, too, but she's worse because she goes around bragging about it.

"There was a fellow named Mock Washington, who had come here from Sumter County. Jackleg lawyer. Big man! Gave to the church, was a Prince Hall Shriner and a Thirty-Third-Degree Mason. He's who Washington Park here is named after. I bet you thought it was named after George Washington, didn't you? He finagled a lot of land from folks, too.

"Anyway, your uncle Sarvis and Mock Washington and Miz Meriwether owned what is now the middle of Gumbo Grove from the ocean to the civic center. The civic center came to be when Miz Meriwether got way up in age and she didn't have any kin to pass her land on to. So she sold five square blocks for thirty thousand dollars to Judge Dyer, who was a buddy of hers. He gave the land to his son, and his son turned around, sold one square block of it for fifty thousand to the city. That's where the civic center sits now.

"Miz Meriwether had a few blocks left, so she willed five or six parcels to her church, Mount Nebo. That way they could build a day-care center. She wanted an activities center, too, where you all could hold your pageant permanently, and not have to try to find a spot for it every year.

"But it goes to show that sometimes our folks don't have a lick of sense here in Gumbo Grove. The Mount Nebo pastor dipped his hand in the till too many times and got the church in all kinds of financial uproar. The congregation finally had to sell most of the property to Judge Dyer to get the church back on its feet. Dyer sold it to the people who own those offices over on Fifteenth Street before you get to the drainage ditch bridge. Church never did get their day-care center or activities wing.

"I told you Miz Meriwether founded the

pageant. She takes care of that pageant to this day from interest off a trust fund she set up years ago just for pageant expenses. And she wrote down how it could be spent and how to run it. That's why the pageant's so popular. It's organized and it's fair. She dearly loved you little girls. She was a smart, proud woman. Very refined. She wanted you all to learn how to be proud of yourselves, too.

"Gumbo Grove and Calvary County girls Black and White were country something awful. We grown women had it hard, too.

"Being a club member and on the committee, I helped Miz Meriwether many times. She taught you to be poised and how to walk properly, not kick your feet out left and right like a mule. She showed you how to put your best side forward and strut your stuff up on stage just as fine as the White girls in their pageants. Back in those days we weren't allowed to mix together the way you and the White kids do now.

"Segregation, Raisin! Plus, we never wanted to be with them, in that regard. We always had our own doings to go to, and they had theirs.

"When Mock Washington got up in years and sickly, his children took turns sitting around his hospital bed, waiting for him to die. Just like vultures. They wanted his money and his property. They would argue and squabble about who was going to get what right in front of him like he was dead already. Mock was old but he wasn't dumb. You don't get to be old being dumb. He cut them all out of his will.

"When the buyers came around to talk to him again, he sold his land to them and then gave the money to Morris College in Sumter and to Fuller Normal and Industrial Institute in Greenville. The land he sold became the mall. The buyers told him they would name that mall after Mock. 'Course, they didn't. They gave us this little park yonder, all overgrown with weeds. Nobody plays there.

"Sarvis was left, surrounded by hotels, the mall, the civic center, and the ocean. That's when the buyers decided it was time for Sarvis to go.

"Judge Archibald Dyer and Dr. Cinch Little came over to see him one day. Dyer owned Dyer's Lumber Company and a bunch of land. Little owned Little's Oceanfront Café. Ole Dyer must have been feeling pretty proud. They'd almost got it all!

"They offered Sarvis thirty thousand dollars. Sarvis said no, because he knew his land was worth way more than that. They got to arguing, and Sarvis made them get off his property. I know, because Sarvis told me this out of his own mouth.

"Things quieted down for a few years. Didn't anybody say anything else about Sarvis's land. But his fishing business fell off. First, all the Whites stopped buying, and then even the Colored people slowed down. This was Dyer's and Little's doings, see. I know for a fact that they threatened to take people's jobs away if they bought fish from Sarvis, Black folks and White folks both.

"Then Judge Dyer came up with a two hundred dollar fishing permit he said Sarvis had to have. Sarvis paid that. Judge said Sarvis also had to have a special boat permit. Another two hundred. Sarvis paid that. That judge threw licenses and permits every which way at Sarvis. Your great-uncle Sarvis must have paid a thousand dollars in licenses, though none of the other fishermen had to. Everybody knew why. Judge Dyer was wrong to do that to Sarvis, but nobody dared stand up to the judge.

"The city health department came along and said Sarvis's building was a health hazard to customers and would have to close down! How could they say that? Because ole Cinch Little was the city health inspector, that's how. His granddaughter is a social worker with the health department now and just as crooked as he was. So they closed Sarvis down.

"But Sarvis still wouldn't sell.

"The way it came down in the end was like this: ole Judge Dyer got so greedy he came back to Sarvis's house and raised Cain again. Sarvis made him get off his property *again.* When Sarvis looked out his back window, he saw Ku Kluxers out there in their sheets, setting fire to everything he had. Sarvis stayed right inside that burning house, grabbed his shotgun, and cut loose on them Klan. And he shot one.

"We found out later that the Kluxer he shot was Sheriff Edgars. He was laid up quite a spell with his shoulder wrapped tighter than a Christmas box. Sheriff said it was a hunting accident.

"I was at home when Deacon Rapture hurried over to tell that the Klan had Sarvis. This was the night Sarvis usually had his oyster roast for himself and his old friends. Deacon Rapture and my Rev would go. I never much cared for oysters. Deacon Rapture was on his way when he saw the fire and the sheets. He turned right around to spread the word.

"Everybody stayed away from the beach that night. Couldn't a soul help Sarvis.

"The next day I listened to the grapevine

and the radio station from over in Deacons Neck. The radio made it sound just like it was Sarvis's fault that he got burned up. The radio said Judge Dyer had gone down to help Sarvis with a legal matter, found Sarvis drunk. Sarvis then supposedly knocked over a lamp, set his own house on fire, and burned up. Shuh. Everybody in the whole county knew Sarvis wouldn't touch so much as a drop of alcohol.

"Later that day Reverend and Deacon Rapture asked the sheriff laid up in the hospital could they collect Sarvis's remains for burial, and he said yes, clean up every scrap. Rev and Deacon and some other burial league members went down there. They picked up the charred wood and piled everything on the burial wagon.

"Then Reverend thought to lift up this big sheet of metal that had been part of Sarvis's kitchen floor. He lifted up that sheet and found himself eyeballing the barrels of a shotgun.

"Sarvis was at the other end of it.

"Talk about who was more surprised, looking death in the face each way!

"Well, it turned out that after he shot the sheriff, Sarvis went down under the floorboards and under that metal into what he called his root cellar. It was really a big ole drainage pipe he had installed under his house when he built it. Just as watertight as it could be, about five feet wide and five feet high. Nobody had known it was there until then.

"Reverend and the deacon were overjoyed to see him alive. Then they got scared over what to do with him, because he *was* still alive. They did know that they had to move quick. They hid him in the burial wagon and without so much as stopping anywhere to get him a change of clothes or wash his face, they hiked out for the North Carolina line.

"They had to be so careful and not rouse any attention. When the deputy sheriff drove up alongside them, they thought their time was up. He drove behind them for about four blocks, and then he turned off. Rev said he started to breathe again.

"Reverend and Deacon Rapture carried Sarvis into North Carolina, and up past Shallotte. Somewhere around up there they let him get out of the wagon and breathe fresh air. Reverend gave him ten dollars, which was good money in those days, and told him good luck and don't come back.

"They said Sarvis stood in the middle of the road staring back from where they'd come. Reverend had to tell Sarvis to go hide in the woods. The man had to been in shock! Wouldn't you be after going through all that?

"Sarvis's land? Dyer put it out that when he came to see Sarvis, Sarvis changed his mind and sold all his property to the judge. Didn't anybody believe that, but in the end Dyer got the land.

"It wasn't more than a month later that I saw some workmen surveying Sarvis's property. Next time I went through there, the main part of that boardwalk you see now had shot up like a dandelion and was open for tourist business.

"Five years later, Sarvis did come back to Gumbo Grove. He came back in a pinewood box from a funeral home up in High Point, North Carolina. Your momma and daddy and a few of us who remembered and who weren't scared came to the cemetery here and funeralized him. Everything was real hush-hush. Didn't want anybody to know that Sarvis hadn't been killed in that fire. It would have come back on us, see.

"People don't like to talk about such things as that happening 'round here 'cause they say nothing can be done about it now. Those were the old days. White people aren't like that now, most of them. But we aren't, either."

My face lit up! "We own part of that beach?"

Miss Effie shook her head. "No, baby, your

uncle Sarvis never got a chance to pass it down. He lost it all."

My brain was whirling. He had it, he lost it, we never got it, but we should have. And I never knew! Now, this was something! I was ready to rush home to tell everybody what we had almost owned. Almost! I frowned up. It should still be ours, shouldn't it? Nobody had the right to steal Uncle Sarvis's property like that!

Miss Effie shook my arm. "What do you think about that?"

"How come nobody told me about Uncle Sarvis? How come Momma and Daddy didn't do anything to help him? Couldn't they have filed lawsuits or something? Daddy always told me he wasn't afraid of anything but the good Lord and a mad woman. The fire, was it in the papers? I want to look it up."

"They didn't have a paper in Gumbo Grove until 1960-something, and the paper in Deacons Neck never printed anything about us unless it had to do with us murdering someone or someone killing us. To the people who ran the paper, Sarvis just burned up, and that wasn't news. You go ask your folks about your uncle."

I was confused. "Why wouldn't anybody

help Uncle Sarvis get his land back? Couldn't he have gone to the police?"

"You're not hearing me, Raisin. The sheriff *was* the police, and he couldn't go to the sheriff 'cause the sheriff ran the Klan. You got to understand some things about Calvary County. Folks up here looked out for me, myself, and I first and for you, him, and them later. Those days—1950s, 1940s, and on back—we were cut off from everybody who could do us any good in the long run. We hardly even made much contact with Charleston or Columbia. There's never been enough of us living here to make much noise. Our so-called leaders, like Miz Meriwether and Mock Washington and them, would be in cahoots with the very same folks who were doing us in, to protect them and theirs. Like Aussie Skipper's trying to do."

I bit my lip, trying not to be angry that nobody helped Uncle Sarvis, and still feeling goose bumps of pride and amazement rise on my arms about us almost owning beachfront property. Well, Uncle Sarvis at least.

Miss Effie pointed at the graveyard. "You see that statue of an angel so weathered with age that it looks green? Right beside that grave is your uncle's grave. I don't recollect that he even still has a marker standing. Sure, some-body should have helped Sarvis, I wish I could have. He was always nice to me."

We sat quiet again. I leaned against Miss Effie, thinking about Uncle Sarvis. Then Momma's and Daddy's warning about Miss Effie saying stuff she wasn't sure about made me sit up straight. How much was true about Uncle Sarvis and how much was, well, made up?

Was there really a Sarvis Exile? Was he actually kin to us? I crossed my legs and folded my arms. I thought I knew who all my kinfolk were.

And the way she talked about White peo-ple made me think she was prejudiced. Momma and Daddy always told us it was wrong to be prejudiced and that we should love everybody. There wasn't any more segregation, either, as far as I could tell. Was there?

"Miss Effie, I got to go home," I said.

"Now, I got you upset, didn't I?" Miss Effie wiped her eyes like she was crying. "I'm sorry. Old woman just rambling on. You don't need to hear about sad stuff. I ought to tell you about Josephine Pickens, our educator. She wasn't much older than you when she began to teach school. She scratched letters in the dirt for children to learn from.

"I ought to tell you about the time Snoop

Vereen found a solid gold parrot figurine in the ground when he was helping to lay city lines back in the 1930s along Cypress Swamp Road."

"Solid gold?"

"Yeah, baby. I'll tell you about that next time, maybe."

5

I couldn't wait to get home and ask my folks
about Uncle Sarvis and the terrible things that
had happened to him—if there was such a
person. That still nagged at my brain, you
know? Miss Effie could have made up that
whole story. Being at her house was like going
into another world, a world that I had only
read about happening in other towns to other
people. Could these things have happened in
Gumbo Grove, too? And it was juicy-sounding
gossip, too!

As I rode my bike along Strom Thurmond
Highway, I watched folks in campers and
station wagons crowded bumper to bumper

rush past me for the beach. I wanted to yell at them that my uncle Sarvis used to own part of that beach. Maybe.

Suddenly I had to go to the bathroom. All that tea! As close to home as I could get was the Fifteenth Street drainage ditch. So I slid into the Gumbo Limbo Soda Fountain and Café yard, dropped my bike in the dirt, hit the screen door, and smashed into old Mr. DeBerry on his way out.

"Excuse me," I said, untangling my arm from his overalls strap. I almost got hung up in the orange streamers that Mr. Easau was stringing from the jukebox to the top of the door.

Sweating and anxious, I flew into the rest room. Made it!

Mr. Easau's rest room was clean, praise the Lord. The one in Miz Camille Stringfellow's restaurant was not. You had to go through a long dark hall with half-closed doors on each side. Old gummy paint cans, broken-up chairs and couches, raggedy quilts, socks, piles of old newspapers, and a nasty, musty smell rose up and surrounded you there. All she had for a rest room door was a curtain. Roaches and centipedes bigger than my thumb crawled all over the floor, which was usually wet. Momma was very strict on telling me where I could put my behind. The toilet seat in Miz Stringfellow's restaurant was not one of them.

When I came out of the rest room, I apologized to Mr. Easau for being so unmannerly. He just smiled and continued to string streamers. I hurried out because Momma didn't like me hanging around inside. I could hang around outside, though.

Junebug and Walter Bill Hill, the peanut boys, sat on the steps drinking chocolate soda. They sold boiled and roasted peanuts in little sacks for seventy-five cents to the tourists and us. Junebug threw out his foot to trip me when I came outside, but I jumped over it like it was just an old stick on the ground.

"Just like a daggone frog," Junebug laughed. He followed me to my bike. "Why'd you throw your bike down like that?" He put a frown on his face and pulled his beret down low over his eyes like he was trying to be bossman. Being a head shorter than me, he had to look up at me, so he didn't make much of an impression.

Just then Big Boy rolled around the corner of the building.

"Your momma let you out again, I see," she said, popping and smacking her gum. She had her radio strapped around her shoulder, and the earphones straddled her neck. She looked like a robot. And an ugly one at that.

When I played like she wasn't even around and instead got on my bike, she walked in front of me and grabbed the handlebars.

"Hey, I ain't bothering you, girl." I looked over to Junebug for help.

"Go home," Junebug told Big Boy.

Big Boy doubled up her fist. "*You* go home!"

Junebug got to his feet, picked up his basket of peanuts, and started to walk up the sidewalk. Walter Bill put his head down and fiddled with his tennis shoe lace.

Some help they were!

Big Boy grinned, showing her gray-brown teeth. "Now, seem like we got some talking to do. Seem like you called me a monkey."

The devil must have got into me right then because suddenly I decided that even if I had to die in the process, I was going to get Big Boy off my back for good. "Girl, you ain't even fresh. Always woofing about nothing. I know stuff about you that you don't even know."

Big Boy stopped grinning. "You don't know nothing. You—"

"Just quit. You are so tired. You're not

even fresh. You don't even know who your people are."

She shook my handlebars. "Look out, Pigeon Face, don't go saying nothing about *my* family." And brought that huge fist up.

Sweet Jesus in heaven! My mouth froze up, and so did the rest of me.

"What do you know? Better tell me before I bust your—"

My mouth unfroze. "You hit me and you'll never know. All this time and you never even knew."

"Never knew what? What're you saying I don't know nothing about?"

"Stop shaking my bike and maybe I'll tell you."

Big Boy pulled her hand off my bike and lowered her fist. I started to breathe again. I backed my bike away from her to the side of the street, but she followed, asking me what I knew. I let her keep asking, but I didn't want to push my luck, either.

"I'm gonna tell you about Gussie Ann Vereen," I said. I told her the story that Miss Effie had told me. "She's kin to you, and you didn't even know."

"You a liar. I ain't kin to no slave. Plus I already heard about that Gussie Vereen and ain't nothing to it. Sure not no connection to me."

I shrugged and pushed off on my bike. When I'd got about ten feet away, Big Boy hollered for me to wait up. "You know so much, show me where she is in the graveyard. I wanna see."

I told her I figured that she already knew. She said she forgot. "I still don't know if I ought to tell you, because you don't act like you got any manners at all. Like, I'm nobody's liar, okay?" I poked out my lips and looked at Big Boy as mean as I could. I was just full of the devil!

Big Boy looked mean back; then she straightened out her face. "Okay."

I almost fell off my bike in surprise.

I took her to the cemetery and told her where she could find the grave. She walked in. "Come with me," she said. "I want to be, unh, exact on where it is." I went in. I figured she didn't know or was scared.

But Big Boy didn't act scared. She jumped right into those weeds and stamped through like nothing that would bite was there. If there was, I hoped it would bite her first. When we came to the little grave, Big Boy looked confused. "This is it? This little pile of dirt?" She stared down at it for a second. "And what was that part about her waiting for her daddy and him not coming?"

"I thought you knew the story."

"Better tell me!" she said. "I mean, I mean, tell me." Then she stopped and just stared at me.

I thought she looked sad, but since I'd never seen Big Boy look anything but mean, I couldn't be sure. Just to be on the safe side, I made her promise to act decent whenever she was around me or my sisters and not to threaten to beat us up. She frowned up for a second, then choked out an okay.

I told her the story again. "And her name was Gussie Ann Vereen. Miss Effie said she was a hero."

"Grandma Skipper never said nothing about me having kin out here," she said. "There wasn't nobody on my daddy's side she ever said anything good about. She said the only people ever amounted to anything came from her side, where my momma came from."

"Well, Miss Effie said she's kin to you, and to your grandmother, too."

Big Boy's eyes widened. "Really? Humm."

Nobody knew where Big Boy's parents were. They say Miss Aussie kept such a tight rein on Big Boy's mother, Tee Ann, when she was a girl that Tee Ann never developed right in her head. She was cross-eyed, too. But when this Gullah-speaking man from the islands around Charleston came through, Tee Ann got straightened up enough in her head and in her eyes to run off with him. He became Big Boy's daddy.

Miss Aussie ran after them. She looked for two years and finally tracked them down. She had given up on Tee Ann, but she thought she would try again with Tee Ann's baby, Big Boy, and brought Big Boy back.

"I didn't know about this slave girl," Big Boy admitted. "I wanna talk to Miss Effie." Big Boy started to high-step through the weeds again. "You come on with me."

"I gotta go home," I said.

"No, you gotta come, 'cause that ole lady don't like me."

"But I gotta go home!"

"Please?"

My mouth fell open when she said please.

Miss Effie looked so surprised when she saw me back at her house, this time with Big Boy. She took us into her parlor, and then she left the room. I looked around for a place for us to sit. The chairs all looked so fragile I got scared wondering which one would hold Big Boy's body and which wouldn't. Big Boy settled the problem; she flopped on the couch.

Miss Effie returned with the tray of pound cake and iced tea. "And how are you today, Big Boy?"

"I want for you to tell me about Gussie," Big Boy said.

"Oh, I see. Didn't your grandmother ever speak of her?" She smiled real kindly at Big Boy.

"No."

Miss Effie told her the story. "And now you know it, too. You got right smart relatives in that graveyard," she went on. "A great-great uncle and a slew of cousins, I expect, on your daddy's side. Your daddy had a lot of kin up here, even though he came from the islands."

"Where?" Big Boy demanded.

"Where what, baby?"

"Where's my daddy's relatives?"

"You mean where are they buried or where are they living? Some of them are buried in that little spot way in the back. The prison plot."

Big Boy scowled and looked down.

"Your grandmother's got kin right there, too," Miss Effie said with a little laugh. "Half of Calvary County's got relatives in the prison plot, but nobody wants to admit it. Let me tell you about some of the people who are kin to you and your grandmother. And everybody else. Raisin, you still got your taping machine?"

Prisoners and Col. Bottom

Told to Me by Miss Effie Pfluggins

June 15

"Race Path was a name given to Negro neighborhoods around here. Oh, some called where we lived Tin Top Alley, Gold Coast Row, the Hole, the Hill. Depending on what went on up in there.

"This particular Race Path in Calvary County was between Deacons Neck on the Deacons Neck side of the Big Sing River. This little place had front porches and all dirt roads. Not an inch of concrete, blacktop, or coquina. The county prison farm was located close by. Every time it rained in Race Path the wagons got stuck so bad! I'm talking about four or five feet of ole muddy dirt road. You couldn't get anywhere! The prisoners on the chain gang would have to go in there and pull out the wagons. Oh, this was back in the 1950s or so.

"They had a real old man on that chain gang. He shouldn't have ever been on it, but that's where he was. He was a preacher who got old and didn't have anybody, so he just wound up at the prison farm. They'd let old Colored men come in without doing anything wrong 'cause there wasn't any nursing homes around for them to go to.

"Well, this ole fella was out in the mud up to his knees one hot, humid day on the chain gang, trying to help them get a wagon loose in Race Path. He had a stroke and died. They used to bury the Colored prisoners just any-where in the woods, but the people in charge of the prison farm felt they couldn't really do that with this ole man. Him being a preacher and not really done anything wrong, you know.

"So the prison thought it would be fitting to bury him in the New Africa Cemetery. Honey, when some of the members heard about that, they had a fit. They didn't want any prisoners buried next to them and theirs! So the burial league set aside a little plot way in the back of the cemetery for this old man.

"That's how the prison plot got started. They kept burying prisoners back there with him. He was kin to Miss Aussie. She could have taken him in, but she didn't. She didn't want anybody to know that he was kin.

"But that was all so silly, because half the men in Gumbo Grove had done time at the prison farm. It got so that a lot of them died out there, too. They were buried in the prisoners' plot. I got a second cousin in there who was such a thief that I was embarrassed any time his name was mentioned. But it was like that for just about everybody. There was always one in everybody's family, Black and White.

"Any time you have a bunch of men around, you're gonna have two or three bunches of women, too. Girlfriends, wives, relatives. Man come up, get in trouble, go to prison, get out. In and out. In and out. The women were a little rowdy sometimes, too. Most of them got jobs washing and ironing clothes, doing day's work, working in the tobacco fields, waiting until their men had served their time and got out. Then they'd leave together. 'Course, some of those fellas stayed in trouble so blessed much that the girlfriends and wives had a long, long wait! They had to settle down!

"Guess where those wild birds settled?

"To the edge of Race Path where they threw up some awful shacks, right by the decent folks! Brought all their rowdiness with them! You should have heard what the regular church-going people said about that!

"That little spot became the roughest place. Cutting, fighting, shooting all the time. Women and men! The decent people were scared to death. The Rev went over there a few times to try to hold services, but them cutters and shooters ran him off. Miz Meriwether even went over there once to try to get the mothers to put their kids in the pageant, and they run *her* off, too.

"Somebody had to do something.

"There come along a Negro detective named Col. Bottom. Old man. He was Miss Aussie's kin some kind of way. Yours, too, Big Boy. He came home from the army where he had been a career man. Col. Bottom weighed near three hundred pounds. Short, bullet-headed fella with a big handlebar mustache and one eye. Wore a black bowler hat and a black three-piece suit. Gold pocket watch and diamond rings. Fancy! He used to be official escort for the girls in the pageant back then. He went in Race Path and slapped so many heads he had Colored folks and White folks, too, running out of Race Path from both ends of the road for a month afterward. He cleaned up Race Path for true!

"As time went on, the other Colored folks moved from Race Path, too. Better jobs came to be, so people could build new homes and get paved streets. They started building up a spot near Deacons Neck. They called it Race Path, too, and that's where they are now.

"And in the spot where that old Race Path was? That's where they built the community college.

"You'd never known that if I hadn't told you," Miss Effie said. "There's things that've gone on in this county that you're never gonna read in any history book and that the Chamber of Commerce surely wouldn't want told."

Big Boy stood up. "I'ma ask Grandma about this Gussie and them prisoners and Col. Bottom," she said. "Seem like she woulda told me who they were if they were kin."

"You ask her; she knows. But she's the one wants to get rid of the cemetery 'cause she's shamed of her own people. Don't be shamed of where you come from. God did that!" Miss Effie half rose from her seat, then sat back down. "I'm sorry. I didn't mean to get loud."

Big Boy was all frowned up, but she didn't say anymore. She just marched out of the room. As we walked onto the porch, Miss Effie took me by the arm. "Oh, Raisin, I want you to look up Alexander Morgan G. Dickson—who he was and what he did."

I shrugged and said okay.

Big Boy jammed her earphones onto her head and stamped up the path. I followed, pushing myself on my bike with my feet, wondering what Big Boy thought about Gussie Ann and the prisoners' plot. Col. Bottom sounded like somebody exciting to know about, but Miss Aussie sure didn't think so!

"People ought to know about their kin-folk," Big Boy finally said. "Ain't that right?"

"What?"

"I said people ought to know about who their kinfolk are, especially if they ain't done nothing wrong. I'm gonna see what Grandma says, and if she says Miss Effie is right, I'm gonna tell everybody about Gussie Ann, and nobody better say nothing off the wall. Else I'll pop 'em one."

"Just as long as you don't pop me," I reminded her.

She grinned. "You all right with me. You might got some sense, after all. We gonna be tight buddies, too." She fell in step beside me like we were friends. I wasn't sure I wanted to be so tight with her, though.

And I wasn't about to ask her what she would do if Miss Aussie said Miss Effie was wrong. I left her by the Gumbo Limbo and, hoping Momma wasn't mad at me, hurried home.

6

Hattie met me at the door, grinning from ear to ear. "I get to be in the Miss Ebony Pageant and you don't," she yelled. "And I get a new dress, and you gotta help me sell ads so I can be queen!"

"What? When?"

"You were over at Miss Effie's when Miss Wilhemena came over with the application forms. This was the last day to apply, and it's too late now."

"Oh, no!" I hurried past her to Momma. "How come Hattie gets to be in the Miss Ebony Pageant and I don't?"

Momma looked up from the couch where

she was sewing on one of Daddy's shirts. "You been at Miss Effie's all this time? It's Sunday evening already."

"Yes, ma'am. Momma, Hattie said I couldn't be in the pageant." I plumped down beside her. "How come? That's not fair."

"You never told anybody you wanted to be in it, but Hattie's been jabbering about it for two weeks."

"I remembered, just up till yesterday, and then I forgot. Momma, I've been saying all year I wanted to be in it. Hattie can't win. But I can. And I know how to get ads. Remember how I tied for first runner-up last year?"

"Then if you're that good, you can help Hattie. You can't be in everything all the time, Raisin. Plus, this will give Hattie a chance to do something. And Lord knows, if any of you children need to do, Hattie do!"

"Shoot!" I jumped off the couch, but Momma grabbed me by the waistband of my shorts and bounced me back down. "Shame on you," she said. "You needn't go get an attitude and blame other folks 'cause you forgot. You're the oldest sister; show some gumption. You help Hattie, and I mean it. And you ain't been at Miss Effie's all this time, so you better be careful how you do."

I shut up. But I sure had wanted to be in that pageant. I tried to keep from screwing up my face with disappointment.

Momma still had her hand on my shorts. "You decide."

It hurt my lips to form the words, but I knew we'd be right here on this couch forever otherwise. "Yes, ma'am," I mumbled. "I'll help. *But it's still not fair.*"

I said that last part inside my head.

Momma said thank you and let loose of my clothes.

"And I'd like to hear those tapes you made today, please," she said. I said okay and gave one to her. Then I stamped out of the room, through the house, and out to the porch steps, where I sat down hard.

No pageant for me. Phooey!

Well, I had promised Momma, so I had to help Hattie. Wasted effort, though. Hattie had the personality of a rock sometimes, and her head was about as hard.

Maizell came out on the steps and sat down beside me. "Momma called Miss Effie about two hours ago to see if you were still there, but Miss Effie said you had already gone. Momma is jawed 'cause you been gone so long. Where you been?"

"I went back to Miss Effie's house after I

told Big Boy about that little girl named Gussie Ann being buried in the cemetery."

"That cemetery's gonna get you in big trouble, just like Momma said. Plus, Momma's mad 'cause she thinks you're out sneaking around with some boy. Maybe even Junebug."

I sniffed. "Momma must not think I got good taste."

Maizell didn't laugh, though. She said when Daddy went up to Mr. Easau's to get a beer, Mr. Easau told him I had been there talking to Walter Bill and Junebug. "And he said you went off somewhere with Big Boy. Last night you were out somewhere with Bunny, and told Momma one thing and did another."

"How'd you know all this?"

" 'Cause Amanda told me she saw you out there last night, and 'cause there were some parents upset about the dance going on so late. And you know how grown folks always talk to each other about what we do."

"So Momma knows something, hunh." Oh, boy.

"Don't she always?"

"What gave Hattie the idea to run in the pageant? Did somebody ask her to?"

Maizell shrugged. "You know Hattie. She's always wanting to be in something just to be in it. Then she doesn't want to be in it. Me, I wanted to be in, too, but I knew only one of us could be in at a time, so I never even asked. I never get to be in anything."

Maizell never asked to be in anything. She liked to dance, but she wouldn't even be in a dance contest.

"How's Hattie gonna get ads?" I said. "That's how you win in the Miss Ebony Pageant, you know, by raising the most money. People give you ads to put in the souvenir book. She doesn't know how to get ads."

"I know how it works. If people want a full-page ad, they have to pay a hundred dollars to the contestant. If they want half a page, it's fifty dollars a whack. A quarter-page is twenty-five, an eighth is fifteen, and a patron is five. Mary Elouise told me the judges can also give you points on the kind of talent you do and how you walk."

I remembered back. "I had lots of businesses last year, but I bet Hattie won't. Plus, you got to have talent, and she doesn't, and you got to have clothes, and she doesn't. Everybody knows Hattie's terrible on clothes."

"Momma said we're supposed to help Hattie," Maizell said. "You sound like you're really, really mad at Hattie."

My mouth fell open. Then I felt shamed.

"It's not her fault, I guess," I finally said. "I just wanted to be in."

"Well, so did I," Maizell repeated. "Anyway, how're we gonna get nice shoes on those big feet of hers? And she won't wear stockings."

"And ain't nobody puttin' none on me, neither." Hattie came out of the house, slamming the front porch screen door. "Momma said I could wear patent-leather flats with lace anklets if I wanted to and wouldn't be nobody's business but my own."

"You could take a little-bitty heel, like a pump," Maizell said matter-of-factly. "You got to put some stockings on them bumpy legs. Chiggers must love your skin."

Hattie bent down and scratched at a scab on her calf until it bled. "Stop scratching! Your legs look like you ran through a barbed-wire fence," I said.

"Y'all just leave me alone." Hattie stamped across the porch and back into the house.

"I don't know about her and Miss Wilhemena," Maizell said. "Hattie won't listen to nobody."

"Maybe we shouldn't have talked so bad about her legs."

"Well, she's gonna have to do something about them bumpy little legs, I swear." We both giggled.

At the sound of a rescue squad siren, Maizell jumped up and ran into the house. She couldn't stand the screech. I stayed outside, though, wishing I could be in the pageant. Momma came out. I could feel her looking down at me. She said, "Hard head makes a soft behind." Then she went back inside.

Well, I knew she had something to say to me! I went into the kitchen to wash the pans still soaking from dinner. That way she wouldn't have to get after me for not doing that.

The telephone rang.

"Miss Aussie," said Momma to the telephone, "why've you got a bone to pick with Raisin?"

I just about died. Miz Aussie Skipper! Time for me to leave! She was the last person in the world I wanted to have calling out my name. Of course, I tried to keep on looking unconcerned, you understand.

"And you say she and Miss Effie done *what* about the slave girl and the prisoners?" Momma turned around to stare at me. "Spreading what kind of tales? I see . . . I see . . . I see."

Momma said unh-hunh a few times, and I began to sweat. "Well now, Aussie, most all of us born in America's got a little slavery in our backgrounds. Oh, we do, too. I already know that story about that child in the graveyard. Anybody who can remember back a ways has heard that story many a time. Ain't nothing secret about it except to you."

Momma got quiet for a minute. "Say *what?*" she hollered. "She *did?*" Then she hung up.

I picked at my thumbnail and waited.

Momma stared at me for a whole minute. "I warned you about paying attention to that bunch of mess Miss Effie be telling you," she finally said. "You got Miz Aussie Skipper upset now about that slave girl story. What in the world did you and Miss Effie tell Big Boy?" She didn't wait for me to answer. "And where have you been for the last two days?"

"Momma, I ain't done nothin', I swear."

"I know you haven't, and what I'm asking is where have you been and what did Miss Effie tell Big Boy?"

"Momma, everything's right here on tape. I swear I ain't said nothing."

Daddy stopped by the living room, but seeing us, he pulled his foot back.

"Wait a minute," Momma said to him. "You ought to hear this, too. She's done it now. She told Big Boy about the prisoners' plot, and now Miz Skipper wants to raise Cain because Miss Effie said everybody had prisoners in their families."

Daddy screwed up his forehead at me. "What? You passing around stuff like that?"

"No, not Raisin," Momma said, praise the Lord. "Miss Effie. Raisin took Big Boy over to Miss Effie's, and Miss Effie's filled Big Boy's head with that stuff. And now Big Boy's running around telling everybody about Gussie Ann and the prisoners' plot."

"But, Momma, Miss Effie didn't tell Big Boy the story that way," I said weakly.

"You be quiet," Momma said. "And Big Boy is all upset because . . . oh, just one thing after another, and Miz Skipper is screeching worse than a cat got its tail in the gate."

Maizell and Hattie slipped into the room and stood big-eared by the china closet.

Daddy saw them. "You girls go right in the other room," he said. He folded his arms. They left. He and Momma turned to me. "You got some talking to do, Miss Stackhouse," Daddy said.

By the time they got through with me, I had promised that I wouldn't do anymore taping and that I wouldn't go over to Miss Effie's. I think I would have promised them anything to keep from getting a whipping.

I hadn't really done anything *wrong*, they said. But Miss Effie had no business telling me about all the folks buried in the cemetery, since their lives wasn't her business to attend to, or mine, either.

"If you want to write a history about people, you should go to their relatives first," Daddy said. His voice got louder and louder. "But as of right now, I don't want you going to anybody. Just let the whole thing drop."

My eyes got puffed and hot from trying not to cry. "Now I can't do anything, and that's not fair. I can't do research, I can't write anything down—why, I can't even be in the pageant."

"Miss Effie is an old woman. We all love her, but she's gone too far. People have a right to privacy about their history," Daddy said.

"Then how can we ever know about it?" I asked. "That's what you told me about Frederick Douglass and Mary McLeod Bethune. When I asked you who they were, you said to go find out."

"Well, this is different." Daddy unfolded his arms.

"Different from knowing about Uncle Sarvis almost getting burned up in a fire and them stealing his land?"

"What!" they both said at once.

"Miss Effie said—"

"That ole woman can't keep anything to herself," Momma hollered. "Raisin, that happened years and years ago about Sarvis. He's just an old man dead and gone." She slapped her palm against her forehead. "Lord knows what else she's drug up."

"How come you didn't tell me about him?"

"Well, Raisin, things are different now," Momma said. "Those were the old ways."

"Look here, girl, we say *what* we want to say to you *when* we want and *if* we want," Daddy shouted. "You got that straight? You don't be telling *us* what to do, and neither can Miss Effie."

He stamped around the room once, and I flinched every time his big boots hit the floor. I'd done it now, for true. I wished they'd just leave me alone. I didn't make things like this in this old town. They were like this when I got here, you know?

Daddy turned around quick and spit words at me: "And you give me all them tapes!"

"Momma already got one," I whispered.

"What did I say, Raisin!" When he took a step toward me with his hand raised, I ran out of the living room to our bedroom.

"You in trouble, Raisin?" Hattie asked.

"Daddy gonna beat her, I bet," Maizell said.

I snatched up my duffle bag. This was unfair! I pulled out the remaining tapes, including the one I made this afternoon about Gussie Ann, which I stuffed in my top drawer.

"*All* of them, Raisin," Momma said, watching from the doorway. I pulled out Gussie Ann's tape from under my underwear and handed it to her with the others. She left.

"Told you you were gonna get in trouble," Hattie said.

I lay down on my bed and put my arms over my face. I didn't have anything now. But I did know this: the way Momma and Daddy were carrying on, Miss Effie must be right about *some* things!

Why did Miss Aussie have to be so touchy? But I guess the way she bragged about how fine her family was and how they came to Calvary County as free people would catch up with her if people found out she had slaves and prisoners in her background. Then she couldn't be a politician. Just like Momma said.

But lots of folks in Gumbo Grove said the same thing about *their* old relatives being so fine and free, too! Maybe some of them weren't quite right in their stories, either.

That gave me a thrill. Would the cemetery history tell me all this?

But then I got a chill. I bet Miss Aussie was awfully mad at me. Would she be able to get me kicked out of school? She had a lot of pull around here, everybody said. I had a terrible thought: Was anybody else mad at me? The list was already up to three!

I jumped up and went into the kitchen where I found Momma listening to Gussie Ann's tape.

"I'm really surprised." Momma turned down the tape recorder. "You *do* have a lot of history here. Things I hadn't thought about for years. What were you gonna do, transcribe all that talking?"

I nodded.

"Lots of work there, baby."

"Yeah, but I won't mind, if I get the chance to do it," I said carefully. She didn't sound mad at me anymore. "Momma—"

"I guess what your daddy is trying to tell you is that folks like Miss Aussie don't care for people to know all their business. Not out in the open like how you got it here."

"Was there a real Gussie Ann?"

"Like I said before, I can't tell you about what all is true because so much of what Miss Effie's talking about was long before my time." Then she shrugged. "But I heard about Gussie Ann so many times it's got to be true. Nothing really unusual about it. There's a Gussie Ann story somewhere in probably every Black family's history around here. That's how it was."

What she was saying gave me hope. I thought I'd give it a try. "So, Momma, can I have the tapes back?"

"Not quite yet."

Shoot! To hide my disappointment, I turned around and got some tea out of the refrigerator, and was about to go back to our room when Momma reached out and took hold of my arm. She gave it a quick shake.

"You're kinda young to be hanging around Big Boy, aren't you?" she asked.

"I haven't been hanging around her."

"You weren't with her at the dance last night at the school?"

"The dance? Unh, I—"

"You didn't leave with her from Mr. Easau's place?"

"I—"

"Were you at the dance?"

"Momma, Bunny—"

"Yes or no?"

I sighed hard. "Momma, I saw Big Boy, yeah, at the dance, but I wasn't with her, but, yeah, I mean I was gonna ask you if I could go. It was like this, see? It was Bunny." I tried to tell Momma the whole thing, but she got tired of listening and went back to giving me the third degree. And then she got hot at me for making her get off the subject of the dance.

When she got through with me she had grounded me.

She wasn't mad because I was at the dance, even though she didn't want me there. No. She was mad because I was there and hadn't told her I was going and didn't tell her where I'd been when I got back. Now, what kind of sense did that make? I was still grounded.

I walked out to the porch and flopped down on the steps. Daddy was out there on the couch. I wondered if he was going to get started on me all over again. But I sat out there anyway. After a few minutes I figured he was asleep, but when I turned around and peeped at him, I could see his eyes staring up at the porch ceiling. I didn't dare say a word, though, because I was liable to end up being grounded for years, the way they were carrying on.

Then I got sleepy and fell asleep against the post. The next thing I knew, the sky was turning purple over the treetops and houses, and the mosquitoes were eating me up. It was just close to nine o'clock, but I staggered into my room and fell out on the bed, wiped out. It had been a long, long day.

It got worse.

It's bad enough to be grounded so you got to stay in the house. But it's awful when they let you out of the house but not out of the yard. Then you see everything, but you can't do anything about it.

Momma said it would show me that I had to be responsible for my actions. Nobody said a word about the cemetery. This punishment was for being at the dance.

So come Wednesday, three days later, I was still a prisoner. I couldn't even go help Momma clean condos at night or help on the truck with Daddy.

I wasn't supposed to have company, either. But that afternoon Bunny came into the yard. Thank goodness Momma and Daddy weren't home.

She came marching into the yard with her behind high up on her shoulders, copping an attitude.

"I ain't staying," she snapped. "You got your buddy Big Boy to run around with now, so I hear." She rolled her eyes at me hard.

"Who told you that? You know that ain't true." We stood in the yard with our faces puffed up, eyeballing each other out of shock.

"Big Boy told me," Bunny said. "She said you all were tight, tight. I don't even care, though. I was just going past, anyway. But you got some awful no account friends."

I tried to think of something nasty to say

back, but I couldn't. "Big Boy's not my best friend. She's not even a friend. After all the times she's got after me?"

"Well, you hanging around her, you're gonna end up being a booster or smoking marijuana or getting pregnant, or wind up in a home somewhere."

"You ought to stop. I ain't having *nobody's* babies till I'm thirty, and old. And you know I don't like Big Boy. You sound just like my mother."

I propped my hands on our fence and just stared off. I was so tired of people being mad at me for no reason.

"Mandy said Big Boy took a bunch of postcards out of the display rack over at the Quik N Go, put them in her pocket big as you please," Bunny went on.

"And what did Mandy and *her* sticky fingers take?"

"She didn't tell me that, but I know she had to take something. She and Big Boy both are criminals from way back."

I giggled before I could hold it back, and Bunny did, too. We looked at each other and giggled again. It felt good.

"I found out some stuff about Big Boy and her relatives," I explained. "After I told her, she tried to get tight."

Bunny said, "Humph." I also told her about Gussie Ann, the prisoners, and Miss Aussie. "Lord Jesus, don't nobody even care," she said. "Just old-timey stuff."

Not mad at each other anymore, we sat down on the tree-stump flower bed. Hattie clumped into the yard with her lip stuck out and her face turned all which way.

"Lordie, what flew up your shorts?" Bunny asked her.

"Leave me alone," Hattie snapped and went into the house. She had the Miss Ebony Pageant ad sheet in her hand.

"I bet she didn't get a single ad today," I said. "She don't know how to ask people. And for talent, she thinks she can stand there and wiggle her behind and call that dancing."

"Lord have mercy, listen to you. You sound like an old woman," Bunny laughed. "When is the pageant? Are you gonna be in it?"

I wished she hadn't asked. "No, I can't. It's right around the corner, but Hattie won't let me help her."

"Do you want to help her?" Bunny asked in a funny voice.

"Sure," I said. My face got hot.

"Then go ahead and help her. Anyway, Deidra told me she has two hundred fifty dollars' worth of ads, and she just started yesterday. Deidra got ten thousand relatives to help her, too, including Miss Aussie."

"Hat doesn't want Momma or Daddy to help her, either. How're you gonna get ads without your folks helping you?" I said as we went into the house after Hattie.

She was slumped on the couch. "I don't wanna be in no stupid pageant," she told us. "You go ahead, Raisin. You want to be in it so bad."

"Why do you say that?" Had she heard Bunny?

"It's just a stupid contest, and I ain't gonna be stupid with the rest of them stupid girls. I'll just wait until the Calvary County Baptist Convention Pageant comes along. I know I can win something in that one."

"You always want to be in something and then want to back out," I said. "What's the matter now?"

She threw the sheet at me. Momma and Daddy had given her a fifty dollar half-page ad, and Miss Effie had given her a fifteen dollar ad, and Deacon Vandross and Mr. Cannon had each given her five dollar patron ads. And that was all!

"Girl, you need help bad." I gave her back the sheet.

"I don't need help," said Hattie, " 'cause I quit!"

"Who quit what?" Maizell came in.

"Look, Hat, you got to raise money if you want to win. It's not hard to sell ads if you know what to say. And even if you don't win, it's fun to do. Bunny, be like I'm trying to sell you an ad, okay? Good morning, ma'am." I smiled sweetly at Bunny and lifted my chin. "My name is Hattie Stackhouse and I am running for the Miss Ebony Pageant because I want to be Little Miss Ebony Queen. I'm selling ads to raise money, and I hope you will buy some space." I rattled off the ad prices. "And I sure will appreciate it, and thank you."

Bunny blinked at me. "Girl, you know I ain't got no money."

I flashed my eyes at her, trying to get her to play along. "You can get money for this. It's all going to a good cause."

"What kinda good cause?" Bunny asked.

"See, she's stallin'. She don't wanna buy, either," Hattie said.

"Guess what I heard today about Deidra and the pageant?" Maizell said.

"That she's got two hundred fifty dollars' worth of ads. We know."

"No."

"Then what?" we all said at once.

Maizell grinned wickedly. "Can't tell. Momma told me not to pass gossip."

"Then I'm gonna tell Momma you got gossip that you're teasing with!" Hattie said.

"I was just playing," Maizell said. Then she grinned again.

We begged and begged her to tell us.

"Okay. Miss Aussie's going around telling folks not to buy ads from anybody except Deidra. That's what I heard Moochie tell Junebug."

"That's not fair!" Hattie shouted.

But I shook my head. "People just say that. Nobody really does it."

"Yeah, but why does Deidra get a fifty dollar ad from Deacon Vandross and Hattie only gets five?" Maizell wanted to know. "I saw Hat when she went up to him. He gave her a five dollar bill, but Miss Aussie came along right behind us, and he gave her fifty dollars for Deidra!"

"Maybe if you went around with your momma and your momma asked, you'd get some ads," Bunny told Hattie.

"Momma brought in the ones I got now, except for Miss Effie's." Hattie glared at me. "You ain't even bought an ad from me, and neither has Maizell. And that ain't fair."

I was embarrassed. "But I will," I said quickly.

"Probably just a little one." She frowned.

I straightened up. "Hey, I won't be giving you a penny if you're gonna sound like you don't even want it. No wonder you don't get any ads. You act too negative. You got to make people want to buy ads."

"Hunh, ain't nobody gonna want to buy ads from an ole evil bear like that," Maizell said.

"But they will from a nice one," Bunny said quickly, finally getting the point. "Hattie, I only got a couple dollars, but I'll see if I can round up an ad from my brother and sisters, okay?"

Hattie's face brightened. "How much?"

"Five dollar one."

"Oh," she said.

"Be glad for that, Hattie!" I said. "Five minutes ago you didn't even have that one. Five dollar ads add up!"

"Thanks," Hattie said to Bunny out the side of her mouth.

"And smile when you thank people, please!"

"Raisin, I can't win with just this five dollar ad," Hattie told me. "I wanna quit." Then she started to cry.

"Don't cry." We crowded around her. "And you ain't dumb at all. So use your brains." I put my arm around her, and Bunny and Maizell did, too. "You use your brains and smile and you can get more ads. Don't be scared! I'll buy one if you ask me nice, and so will Maizell."

I cut my eyes at Maizell, who was about to say something. "We'll all help if you let us."

Maizell wanted an ad, but she didn't want to pay, of course. I had to pinch her to make her say yes.

Things went a little better after that, for me at least. Helping Hattie took my mind off being grounded, a little. I missed talking with Miss Effie. What would happen next? Would they go ahead and move the cemetery? What if Miss Aussie managed to sell it without anybody knowing? Suddenly I remembered what Miss Effie had told us about losing land because of no deed. Was there such a thing as a deed to a cemetery? And who had it? Not Miss Aussie, I hoped!

Meanwhile, Thursday and Friday went by. By Saturday I began to see an improvement in Hattie. Praise the Lord. She started to act nicer to people, which made people act nicer to her. We would sit out on the porch and watch for people to walk past our house or go into Johnson's Barbershop across the street. Then Hattie would stop them and give her little speech. Or she'd go over to the barbershop. Folks bought ads more times than not!

She learned not to frown up her face when people hesitated or said no. By Monday she had $145 worth of ads and another $50 in pledges.

I also had her call folks up on the telephone and ask when she could come over.

Now the big test was what was she going to do for talent? When I asked her, you know what she said?

"Tell jokes and do gymnastics."

Maizell rolled. "You get out on stage and break your neck trying to do flips. You can't even walk straight!"

Hattie got huffy over that. "I can tumble and stand on my head and do the splits!" she declared.

"You can't do any of them good enough to do in a pageant. Lemme hear you do a joke."

"You know good and well Momma's not gonna let you tell jokes," I told her. "You got to dance or sing or play the piano or give a monologue or something."

"If I can't tell jokes, then I ain't gonna be in it," Hattie said.

"Then you better give back all that money right now," I reminded her. I took my book of poems off the bookcase by my bed. "You could read a poem. It'd have to be—"

"I won't!"

"—at least three minutes long. You could memorize parts of it and dramatize it."

"No!"

Ignoring her, I turned to "For My People" by Margaret Walker, my favorite, and began to read the poem to her. "Can't you just see yourself acting out parts of this, Hattie?"

"No, I ain't ever gonna see myself wanting to act out cooking and scrubbing when I gotta do it for real," she said.

"Yeah, but you don't do it for real, either," Maizell said, giggling.

I waved at Maizell to be still, and began to act out how to cook and iron and scrub.

At least Hattie watched. "But I still ain't gonna do that, and you can't make me," she said when I stopped. "I don't wanna say poems. I wanna tell jokes."

"Your show, kid." I got disgusted and left the room. I sat down by the telephone.

Things were so boring around here. And Hattie wasn't making it any easier. Being grounded was the pits, you know? Darn that Miss Aussie!

When I began to remember some of the people Miss Effie had told me about, the name Alexander Morgan G. Dickson popped into my mind. Quickly I picked up the telephone and called the library.

Miz Constance Pennyfeather, the head librarian, answered. "I was just saying to Miz Rodriguez the other day that Raisin must be sick 'cause I hadn't seen her in here all week!"

"Well, unh, yes, ma'am. Miz Pennyfeather, do you know who Alexander Morgan G. Dickson was?"

"The name doesn't ring any bells. Know what he did? Was he military? Is he alive or dead? Got any hints for me at all? You forget I'm from Pennsylvania, though I've been here thirty years, and am not all that up on the minor points of South Carolina history. Though I did get that plaque from the Historical Society for—"

"I don't know anything about him except that Miss Effie said for me to find out who he was. I think he's local, and I think maybe he's been dead for a while, 'cause when she told me, we were talking about the cem— I mean, talking about things."

"Well, let me chew on him for a while. If Miz Rodriquez was in, I'd ask her, but she's off today. If I have to, I'll call down to the Charleston County Library. They know everything. Or I'll call Columbia."

I listened politely, hoping Hattie or Maizell wouldn't catch me on the telephone and tell Momma. Miz Pennyfeather said she'd call me back if she found out anything. I hung up. Whew!

The telephone rang right after that. It was Miss Effie! She sounded out of breath. "You gotta come over here right away," she said.

"But I'm—I can't leave the yard. I'm not even supposed to use the telephone."

"This is too important for you to have to stay home for," she insisted. "Put your momma on the phone."

"She's not here," I said. "She had to go clean—"

"Who's not here?" Momma walked into the living room and about gave me a heart attack. How long had she been here? Did she know I'd been on the telephone before? "Is that for me? Lordie, it's hot! I had to walk home today, and my feet are killing me!"

She flopped down on the couch, fanning herself. I gave the telephone to Momma, and she and Miss Effie talked. When she was through, she told me I could go over there "just this once. But don't tape anything about that cemetery, you hear? You two get together and you upset the whole town."

"What's Miss Effie want?"

"I don't know, probably some kind of errand. But you hurry up and get over there and get back, and no foolishness. You're still grounded, you know."

I hopped on my bike. Freedom! Everything looked so tempting. Like the Gumbo Limbo and the mall. I played it safe and made a beeline to Miss Effie's, but my eyes bugged out in all four directions, trying to cram all the sights in.

I hit the black horsehead knocker on Miss Effie's front door three times hard, like she always said to do, but nothing happened. Was she sick when she called? Had she fell out in the house? I ran around the house and pounded on the back door. No answer. I ran to the front and tried again. I remembered how ole Miss Green fell out in her house when she had a heart attack. She lay on her kitchen floor three days before anybody found her.

Just as I was about to go to the back door one more time, Miss Effie opened the front door.

"Child, you got me flying from one end of the house to the other trying to open doors for you."

"Where were you?"

"I was back in the study and couldn't get up here quick as usual."

She led me to her study. It was a stuffy little room filled with shelves of books and papers. Boxes were piled on the floor and on tables and clustered on the couch.

"They're trying to do me so wrong, but the Lord will punish 'em," she said. "Sit down anywhere you can find space, Raisin."

She handed me two large, dusty green books. "Open 'em. Read 'em. Keep hold to 'em so she can't get 'em."

I opened the book marked Volume One and Two. My mouth fell open. It was the minutes of New Africa No. 1 Missionary Baptist Church! The first entry, in flowery, faded handwriting, was dated October 7, 1878! That was when they first began to keep records.

"Oh, Miss Effie!" Cautiously I turned the thin, brown pages, afraid they would tear or crumble in my fingers. "But I can't take these. They belong to the church, don't they?"

"You got to, Raisin. They're going to call a meeting, and Aussie Skipper and her bunch are going to try to vote me out of being secretary and vote her in instead. If she gets hold of those books she'll change so much in them that nobody will ever know what the real history was. I won't be around forever to remember, you know. And even I forget sometimes. Those books right there are the only Black history books Gumbo Grove has, see! We can't let her get hold of 'em! You got to read 'em and know."

She told me to turn to the back of Volume One and Two. "There's the roll call of the cemetery. The names of everybody buried are there up to 1924, I believe. And the other book follows up on the roll call, right up to the last person buried in the cemetery. It lists all of them, people known and unknown."

"Does it list Alexander Morgan G. Dickson, too?" She nodded. "Who was he, Miss Effie?"

"You tell me, Raisin. Now, you promise me you'll keep these books secret. Not tell anybody."

I hesitated. "But if my folks ask, what should I do?"

"Nobody's going to ask you if they don't know. Plus, as long as Miss Aussie can't get the books I don't figure she can be secretary. That'll give us time to write the history of the cemetery the way it ought to be, save that history."

"But Momma says I can't tape you anymore."

"You don't need to." Miss Effie frowned.

"You got the books now. Write the history from the records. See, if you write from the records you might can save the cemetery, too. People see who all's in that cemetery, like Dickson, they'll want to save it."

"But who is this Dickson, Miss Effie?"

She just smiled. "If you're going to be a history teacher you got to do research. See, I can't trust grown-ups. They're too wrapped up in what people think!"

She told me that death notices had been written in the records on many of the people, which would be most helpful, too. "Now you go home and read those books. Tell your momma you had to help me wash the dishes." She gave me fifty cents and then slid the books into two big paper sacks and put them in one of her canvas shopping bags. I took the bag, wondering how in the world I was going to get it into the house without anybody seeing it. And what would I do if I got caught with the books? And where could I keep them safe? And how was I going to get them home on my bike?

"Did Hattie tell you I gave her an ad? I'm sorry you're not going to be in this time, but you'll be a big help to her," she said as I left.

Clutching the books, I said, "Yes, ma'am," but I wasn't thinking about Hattie and the pageant right then. I was so excited I could've screamed! History at my fingertips!

I walked the bike and the books home. Instead of going directly into our house, I took the books into the shed out back and, hoping nobody saw me, carefully hid them on an upper shelf behind some paint cans, until I could get back to them later.

When I got into the house, Momma asked me what Miss Effie wanted. I told her it was to wash dishes.

"And that was an emergency?" She frowned, eyeing me. "Oh, the library called. Miz Pennyfeather wants you to call her."

My heart jumped, but I tried not to let Momma see me get excited. I made myself sit down and watch television for a few minutes before I asked permission to call. Still watching me, Momma said yes.

"Raisin, you got me so curious that I wanted to know who this Alexander Morgan G. Dickson was, too," Miz Pennyfeather told me. "I spent the rest of the afternoon chasing after that man!

"Well, according to the minutes of proceedings of the Gumbo Grove City Council— 'course they didn't call it that back then—this Dickson was the founder of Gumbo Grove! How do you like that? And he was also the first mayor! Back then there wasn't much to Gumbo Grove but swamp and sand. And he owned just about all of that. He had a little grocery store, a tavern, and a post office at the crossroads of where Strom Thurmond Highway intersects with Ocean Boulevard. That crossroads was just a horse path back then. I'm talking about when Gumbo Grove was struggling back in 1842, when it was founded."

"How come there aren't any signs or plaques or anything about him being the founder?"

"Well, not all towns put a lot of praise on the founders. This Dickson could have been a pirate," she laughed. "That *G* stands for Grove. And listen to this. He had a nickname: Gumbo. They used to call him Gumbo Dickson. Isn't that funny?"

"Boy, you sure know a lot. Could you copy that part about him so I'll have it?"

"Sure. When will you be in?"

When I told her I was grounded, she laughed and said she'd slip it in the mail for me.

Gumbo Dickson? Mayor and founder of Gumbo Grove! I was really puzzled then, because if he really was the founder, why didn't more people know about him? They sure didn't tell us anything about him in school.

And why in the world would he be buried

in New Africa's cemetery? I frowned and puzzled over the whole thing. Why? Unless he was
Black?

Naw. I remembered Miz Gore's words.
Nobody Black around here had done anything
good enough to be famous.

Or had they?

7

Miss Effie must have known all along. Of course! The founder of Gumbo Grove was Alexander Morgan G. Dickson, who was buried in our cemetery. Our history. And everybody's history. No wonder she wanted to save the cemetery so badly! And the books, they—oh, I'd forgot all about them. I jumped up and ran smack into Momma fixating on me with some for-real, serious eyes.

"What are you up to?" She raised an eyebrow at me. "You got that look on your face that says you've already been into some devilish thing or you're about to be—again. And what did Miz Pennyfeather want?"

I got to stuttering. "I just, unh, wish I

could go to the library, and probably Miz Pennyfeather missed me. So she just called, like she does sometimes, you know?" I stretched, asking myself how I'd got to be such a good liar. "And Miss Effie had a lot of dishes. Lordie, I'm tired."

Watching Momma out of the corner of my eye, I sat back down on the chair as if I hadn't planned to go anywhere. "Hattie all ready for the pageant?"

"You mean you don't know? Where you been? She's the same, putting up a battle over everything. She didn't even want to wear stockings until I made her count every chigger bite on her legs and she came up with fifty-seven! Still fighting over what her talent's gonna be, too. Girl, I ain't goin' through this pageant stuff again with *her*, and that's the truth. I've still got to get her dress and shoes and everything, and she's being just as ornery as she can be. If she wins first prize—ha!—it won't even begin to cover the expenses we got just getting her basics. If she'd just get into the right attitude, that would help." Momma got to throwing her arms around in the air.

"I don't know why that child wants to be in this pageant so bad. It must be because you were in it last year. She wants to do everything you do. But if I had to choose between spending a hundred dollars on a pageant dress and putting it away for her college I'd sure Lord stick that money in the bank. The little ones Hattie's age don't even win a hundred dollar prize. Just a radio with headphones that cost no more than fourteen or fifteen dollars, a two-bit trophy, and some flowers. The entry fee costs more than that!"

"Yeah, but it makes you want to try again, Momma, and you learn how to walk like a model, and you get to be around other girls from all over the county," I reminded her.

I knew Momma was fussing because she was worried that Hattie wouldn't make a good showing in her ads and talent. So I just nodded my head while she fussed on. Then I got up and slipped off to the kitchen. I slid out the back door into the dark shadows of the hedges. Carefully watching the kitchen window and door, I opened the shed door just a crack, slipped in, and locked the door.

In a corner was Daddy's tool table, which he hardly ever used after he sliced off part of his third finger with the jigsaw. Above the table a small light bulb hung from a cord draped over the rafter. This made a perfect spot for reading, away from Maizell and Hattie, who said the place was too spooky for them. Plus, it had rats, which I didn't much care for either, but I left them alone, and they did the same with me, so it all worked out.

First I went to the shelf to get the books, nervously wondering if I'd only been day-dreaming that Miss Effie had loaned them to me. We'd made a deal, I told myself, and she'd been fair and square. But I was so nervous! Those books were historical and valuable! And what would I do if they really weren't there?

They were.

The first few pages in Volume One were filled with lists of names of people pledging money for something: Delphine Butterfield, seven cents; Lancaster Grice, ten cents; Prince McKnight, ten cents . . .

Then there were minutes of a meeting. First a Mr. Octavius Bellamy was honored. He was honored because even though his wife had been bed-sick with consumption for the past three years, he still had attended every special call meeting. I wondered what consumption was.

Then there were more names and numbers, page after page after page. I got impatient and thumbed through the book until my eyes caught a blur of yellow. It was a flower that had been pressed between the sheets so long that its petals were stuck to the paper. Beneath, in spidery writing, were these words:

The Lord has brought together
In His highest Holiness
On this date of October 10, 1878
Licentiate Ulysses Grant Thomas
and
Miss Marthena Cody Gaithers

This was the first wedding ever held at New Africa. Great! But that wasn't what I was looking for. After about half an hour of more stuff—babies-being-born notices, more meeting notices, more wedding notices—I started to frown. Where was the good stuff? But I read on: "On February 16, 1887, the New Africa Burial League met at the home of the chairman, Mr. Cephus Stackhouse, for a discussion about the placement of a new marker at the grave of Mr. Gumbo Dickson."

Bull's-eye! I sat up quick and reread the passage.

The older marker had been destroyed by fire ants, the notes said. This Mr. Stackhouse— who had to have been some kin to me, I was sure—made a motion to place a granite tombstone at the grave, being as how Mr. Dickson was founder of Gumbo Grove! But Mr. July Jones argued against putting such a prominent and expensive tombstone there, his point being that such a stone would draw attention to the location of Mr. Dickson's grave and cause "extended negative emotion amongst the White people."

Extended negative emotion?

Why would White people get upset about a tombstone? I thought back. Maybe it had to do with what Miss Effie had told me about segregation. In the old days they might not have liked the idea of a Black man being mayor, let alone founder, of their town. But if that was true, who could have voted him into office?

I was confused about that part. And would White people be bothered about the founder being Black if they were told now? Wouldn't they just be proud of even having a founder?

And shouldn't Black people be proud, too? Or would they? Especially if they remembered he was buried in a run-down, raggedy grave-yard that hardly anybody seemed to want to have around in the first place? Would they be embarrassed?

Oh, Lord . . .

That's when I began to realize that there was much more to being a historian than I'd ever figured. Maybe I would stir up a lot of trouble and make people, White and Black, have buckets of "extended negative emotion" against me if I kept fiddling around in people's stuff. Maybe I wasn't ready for something as heavy as this. Maybe I'd be better off if I left things alone, like Momma and Daddy said.

"Raisin!"

Momma! Was that a sign? Quickly I pushed the books back into the sacks and into Miss Effie's shopping bag, and returned them to the shelf. I hoped Momma wasn't on her way out here. Running to the door and unlocking it, I yelled that I was coming.

When I got to the house, she had her eye on me funny again. "You got company. Big Boy. On the front porch. And a phone call from—"

"Big Boy? What's she want?"

Half scared about Momma and half scared over Big Boy, I walked out to the front porch. There she was. Squeezed into Ocean Pacific shorts and a Panama Jack size small (I'm sure) T-shirt, she stood there looking like a tube of sausage.

"What's goin' on?" she drawled. Her gold tooth sparkled in the light. With her gray teeth, that gold one looked like all she had. "C'mon, girl, let's go down to the Pavilion."

"Now?" Me go someplace with her? She'd never even been to my house before until now. "Naw."

"C'mon, let's go. You can have some for-real fun." She popped her gum. "You and me's tight, remember? We friends. I'm a show my friends how to have some fun, you dig? I seen a dude down there had his head shaved. One bald side was painted green and the other was painted red. He had on a fur vest and purple—"

"Raisin can't go down to the Pavilion this late," Momma said from behind the screen door. "And you ought not to either. Your grandma know where you are?"

"She don't care." Big Boy looked ugly.

"I said, do she know where you are?"

"I don't know. But I ain't a baby."

"Well, Raisin still can't go. And you ought to go home." Momma eyeballed Big Boy like she was about to throw her off the porch.

I said, "See ya," and went back into the house. Big Boy stood on the porch for a few seconds; then she jumped off into the darkness.

"Momma, you made her think I was a little kid the way you talked," I said. "I'd already told her I didn't want to go."

"Well, excuse me, but I thought you'd rather be talking to Bunny than to her. Bunny's been waiting on the phone a good ten minutes. I been hollering for you at least that long. I thought you told me you weren't running around with Big Boy."

She told me that Miss Effie had called, too,

to say that the church planned to vote on new officers one night real soon. I was horrified. That's what she'd meant about Miss Aussie and her bunch and giving me the record books to hide! "Momma, what if they vote her out?"

"It'll be too bad, but these things got to happen to everybody sometimes, honey. And all that stink about the cemetery didn't help her none. People's talking about it all over town. Plus, she's old, Raisin. When you get old you gotta give some things up."

My face wrinkled up, but I went to the telephone.

"Raisin, I thought you'd left town," Bunny complained.

"We gotta talk." I cut her off. "Meet me in the shed in half an hour. Keep quiet, too."

I waited, then crept outside. Something grabbed me! "Argggh!" I about wet my pants.

"Thought I was a ghost from that ole graveyard, didn't you?" Bunny showed her face. "Girl, you so chicken!"

"You ought to quit." I thought my poor heart would rattle right out of my chest.

We went into the shed, and she sat beside me in the armchair as we thumbed through the old record books.

"Don't these books belong to the church?" Bunny asked. "Couldn't the church have you arrested for concealing stolen property or something?"

"But this guy was the founder and first mayor of the town! It's right in the books here, Bunny. Miss Effie can save the cemetery. See, that's big news!"

"You ain't making no kind of sense. Save the cemetery from who? Miz Skipper and Big Boy? I oughta put you on the bus with a man in white and ship you to the state mental hospital. You gotta get your brains outta that grave stuff and come back to the living."

She grinned sly. "Hey, let's shoot down to the Pavilion."

"Big Boy came over and wanted me to go down there, too, not more than an hour ago."

"Oh, that's right; you got that new runnin' buddy, hunh."

"No, girl! But what's down at the Pavilion on a Monday night? I been down there at night before."

"Yeah, but only hanging out the back of your daddy's truck, looking like the Beverly Hillbillies. You being in a car with some fine guy going down there is different. Or being down there with me is different. The stores are all lit up, people be loose, wearing funny clothes, acting stupid, you know? There's lotsa music and noise and colors. Boys be head-spinning on the steps of the wax museum. Can you check out smelling popcorn and orange pop and hot dogs and listening to Tina Turner and seeing purple and yellow lights in the middle of the night all at the same time? It's fun!"

"You want my father to kill me for sure, don't you."

"What he don't know won't hurt him and won't hurt you either. C'mon!"

"So I can be grounded for life, hunh." But I thought about it for a few seconds. Then I looked down at the record books. "And you think I'm crazy, trying to find out about history?"

"Not crazy about history." She shook her head. "Just crazy about cemeteries. You sound like an ole woman. Come on, Raisin. We can fly down there and be back in two hours. Won't nobody even know you're gone. Just act like you're going to bed; then get back up in ten minutes if everything's quiet. I'll be waiting for you out here. Don't take too long. If you think you won't get out or don't nobody want to go to bed in ten minutes, flip the back light on and off two or three times so I'll know you can't go."

"What about Pooch and them?"

"They 'sleep. C'mon!"

"Unh, make it twenty minutes, okay?"

Well, the devil was trying to get into me again. I sure didn't want to sound like an old woman. Between that cemetery and being grounded, I guess I was ready for either the nursing home or the funeral home. So I said okay.

Bunny and I put up the books, and I went into the house, yawning loudly. Daddy was in bed, for once. I knew, because I could hear him snoring. From their bedroom Momma called out, drowsy, "That you, Raisin?"

I said yeah and yawned again loud, then went into our bedroom. When I heard Hattie and Maizell snoring, I knew nothing would wake them up, except maybe sunlight. Twenty minutes later I was with Bunny, cutting through Miz Queen James's back yard, running alongside her rosebush hedge.

We took the trail everybody used to get to the business strip—through the fields behind the Holiness Church. In the distance I could see the giant Ferris wheel slowly turning against the black sky.

We got to Timber Oakes Avenue. Bunny hopped up and down. "Lotsa people still out, see! Look at these cars just flying. We gotta get across this street right, else we'll be here all night."

"We don't do it right we'll be dead in the middle of it," I reminded her.

"You still talking about death, and I am tired of hearing you talk about death to me," Bunny snapped.

I made a promise to myself not to talk about death or graves or cemeteries ever again.

We timed ourselves to zip across the street at the first sign of space in traffic. "Go!" Bunny screamed.

Zoom!

We scrambled onto the median strip, breathing hard, and got ready for the next run. "Go!"

Zoom!

That got us to the parking lot of the Quik N Go Grocery, which was right down the street from Ocean Boulevard and the Pavilion. In the parking lot were four guys in black pants, vests, no shirts, and tattoos on their chests. One of them had a red feather hanging from his right ear. They stood by their motorcycles, drinking beer and smoking marijuana. I knew it was marijuana because the wind was blowing from the east off the ocean, and it blew the smoke right into my nose.

When they saw us, they said something nasty.

Bunny screamed at them. Then she took off around the store and into the alley, me hot behind her. Feet pounded behind us. They were hot after us! I pictured my body being found under somebody's beach house and my head out on the beach a block away. This was fun?

We ran between cars, around palmetto trees, through back yards, and across parking lots. But those ugly Neanderthals stayed just as hard on our trail. Bunny skidded in the coquina and cut back around some pyracantha bushes, which was a mistake. Talk about thorns snatching and scratching! But we struggled on through.

"Bunny!"

"Shut up!"

She made a sharp right turn into a narrow, pitch-black alleyway and darted into a thin doorway. I squeezed in right after her. My legs and behind and arms burned from thorn stabs, and my lungs burned so bad I was sure smoke was pouring out my ears.

I tried to talk, but my brains had to deal with some oxygen first.

We waited in that tiny hot slot for what seemed like forever. Finally Bunny told me to look out in the alley and see if it was safe.

"And get shot in the head?"

"If you don't look we won't know if they're gone. So look!"

I stuck my hand out and waited for my fingers to get shot or chopped off, but nothing happened. Cautiously I peeked into the alley. "I don't see anything."

"Good."

"Bunny, is this supposed to be fun?"

"Yeah."

The tinny bugling of "Oh, I wish I was in the land of cotton" from a musical car horn near Octopus Pete's Aquarium and Museum blared out a welcome to us as we walked down the middle of the street toward the Pavilion. A gang of people dodged cars and bicycle riders in the street, too. One old man and woman in matching Hawaiian shirts, white Bermuda shorts, and thongs tried to stop people. The woman pulled at Bunny's arm, but Bunny pulled away. "Hey, miss," the woman said in a Yankee accent.

"Don't say nothing to nobody!" Bunny warned me. "Lotta these people are *nuts*."

"Please, dear," the woman said. "Which way is the Banner Hotel?" Remembering Bunny's words, I didn't say anything, but I did point north.

"The first thing you gotta learn down here

with me, girl, is how to follow instructions,"
Bunny grumbled when I caught up with her.
"Don't you say *nothing* to *nobody* or point, nei-
ther!"

Colorful blinking and streaking store signs
tinted everything and everybody yellowish orange in the hot night air. We mingled with
people thronging the sidewalks past Murray's
Beachwear, whose doors were wide open. Rock
music rushed out, with the sharp, sweet smell
of strawberry incense. Racks of T-shirts set
outside, where hard-eyed salesgirls in hot pants
and cut-off T-shirts watched us go by. As we
passed, music blared louder, then faded from
record stores, gold and silver jewelry shops,
shooting galleries, photo studios, and cotton
candy shops. Everywhere there were posters
and banners publicizing the Miss Cherry Bomb
Beauty Pageant, Miss Fourth of July Beauty
Pageant, and the Miss Best Body on the Beach
Pageant. I didn't see any signs for the Miss
Ebony Pageant, though.

I stopped in front of Zeno's Ice Cream
Parlor to stare at the heaping bins of Oreo,
pistachio, chocolate peanut butter, and rasp-
berry ice cream, starving to death—I mean,
going nuts, wanting some.

But Bunny pulled me away. "First we gotta
go see them fools get thrown off the bronco

machine. Then we eat. You haven't seen it? It's a weird ride, girl. A person could get killed on that thing. You stay on for about three minutes if you are really lucky. Then you get back the money you paid to ride it. But I only seen three guys do that, and I been watching it for two summers."

What kind of thrill was that? To pay five dollars so you could get thrown off a machine? That didn't even have a tail or a mane? I bumped against a guy with waist-long hair and a black circle drawn around his left eye. He had an earring in his left ear with a large nail hanging off it. I wondered if his earring was pierced or clip-on.

We walked toward a girl in a floor-length black gown; she had black hair and a green face. She stood outside the Chamber of Horrors building passing out brochures. Her mouth was smeared with bright red lipstick. I started to smile at her until she opened her mouth and showed me two fangs. Girl, I got over onto the street side of the sidewalk and away from her!

"Vampire-looking thing, wasn't she?" Bunny said.

A shrill, whiney voice made us stop and look around to where a bright yellow light lit up in the shape of a horse flickered on and off. "Who's ready to break the bronco?" the shrill voice asked.

A skinny, short guy with a Miss Cherry Bomb Beauty Pageant cap on squeaked and squeaked into a megaphone. He wanted folks to ride the bronco.

The "bronco" was just a metal seat with a saddle and stirrups. It was attached to a stout pole that set about four feet off the canvas floor. A husky guy in a cowboy hat, boots, and a John Wayne T-shirt hopped onto the platform. He handed Mr. Cherry Bomb Hat some money and then swung onto the saddle. He tightened his right hand around the handle of the saddle and raised his left arm. Then he waited.

When Mr. Cherry Bomb Hat pulled a lever, the bronco took off. The guy on it started out with a big grin on his face, but the faster the bronco shook him, the smaller his smile got. When the bronco began to jerk his body back and forth like it wanted to shake him to the moon, his mouth got O-shaped. His head snapped back and forth like a puppet's.

To me, this guy was wacko, you know?

"Whoooee, ride 'em, cowboy!" Mr. Cherry Bomb Hat squealed.

Plop!

John Wayne landed on his behind in a

puff of dust. Everybody laughed. Red-faced, the guy got up and, shaking both fists in the air above his head like a boxer, hobbled away.

Another guy tried. Same thing.

"We better move on if we're gonna get back home soon, Bunny." I was bored.

But Bunny grabbed my arm and pointed. "Big Boy!"

There was Big Boy on the platform. Mr. Cherry Bomb Hat shook his head. Big Boy raised her fist and shook it at him, then handed him some money. The man took it. He picked up his megaphone. "This gal here say she legal 'cause she's fourteen and can ride the famous buckin' bronco. So I ain't gonna say no. But anybody get on the famous buckin' bronco get on at their own risk!"

"She is some crazy," I told Bunny.

"I thought you knew that," Bunny said back. "I ain't never seen any women get on that thing."

Big Boy climbed on, wrapped the reins around her arm, and worked her big feet into the stirrups. After squeezing her fingers around the saddle, she held her other arm high. The bronco began slowly, then picked up speed. Big Boy's head bobbed back and forth, faster and faster. Soon her whole body was jerking. She let loose with a yodel that turned into a roar, sounding like how I figured a starving alligator hollered when he saw meat on the way.

Hard to the left, then hard to the right, the bronco jerked faster, but Big Boy yodeled and hung on. People began to clap and whistle at her. Bunny and I did, too. The bronco pitched and churned! Big Boy's mouth went wide, wide, but she pitched and churned right with it.

Finally the bronco slowed and stopped. Big Boy climbed off and, walking wobbly, went over to Mr. Cherry Bomb Hat, who held up five one-dollar bills and handed them to her.

"She beat the bronco!" Bunny said.

Big Boy came off the platform grinning, and everybody crowded around her for about thirty seconds. Then they settled back to watch the next rider. She stood in the sand by herself, looking around to see if anybody else was going to congratulate her, I guess.

"I bet that's why she comes down here," Bunny said, "to get attention. Look at her cheesin' and grinnin' up at people, trying to get them to pat her on the back. Ain't that sick! 'Course she doesn't have any friends at home. Except you," she added slyly.

Big Boy saw us. "Hey, y'all," she said, strutting over.

"Oh, Lordie, we shoulda gone on," Bunny whispered.

"Now you all seein' a champ!" Big Boy said. She eyed me hard. "Thought your momma wouldn't let you out."

"What Momma don't know won't hurt her," I said back just as hard. "How'd you learn to ride like that?"

She shrugged and strutted some more. "Comes natural 'cause I'm good."

Bunny grunted. "C'mon, Raisin. Bye, Big Boy."

"Where you all goin'?"

We just shrugged.

Big Boy got to wolfing. "Did y'all see me ride that bronco! Didn't I ride 'em? Everybody was clappin' after me! Didn't I ride 'em good?"

"Yeah, Big Boy, you sure 'nough did. C'mon, Raisin," Bunny said.

"Y'all ought to get me some ice cream! I'm the champ! Go cop me some chocolate peanut butter in a sugar cone, Raisin."

I just looked at her.

"Go get something for the champ, I said."

"Go get something for us!" I said back, wondering if the "new" Big Boy had fallen back into her "old" Big Boy ways. "You ought to be buying, if you're a champ, like a hero. Like Gussie Ann."

"Who's Gussie Ann?" Bunny said, jealous.

Big Boy stared at me. "Oh. Yeah. Me, a hero? Yeah, I'm the champ! Yeah, and you better believe it, too! Yeah, that's right. Gussie Ann my kin, and I can do like I please. But Grandma said we ain't got no prisoners in our family! Hunh! What you all want? I'm buying!"

We went into Zeno's and jostled up to the counter. I hoped Big Boy wouldn't change her mind about paying and embarrass us, because I didn't have any money on me. When she pulled out three one-dollar bills and gave them to the clerk, I breathed a sigh of relief.

Five minutes later, the three of us walked down Ocean Boulevard eating and gossiping like we were big-time buddies. Well, Big Boy and I did. Bunny wouldn't talk to her. She'd just talk to me. We window-shopped for a while and then sat on the wide steps of Ripley's Believe It or Not Museum, watching the guys and girls and everybody go by on foot, on bicycles, and in cars.

Big Boy spoke up. "Grandma said she didn't care what Miss Effie said about Gussie Ann, and she said I shouldn't never mention her name again. But I done it, hunh."

"Who is this Gussie Ann?" Bunny asked me.

I started to remind her, but Big Boy broke in. "She *my* kin, I'll tell it," she said, and told Bunny the story. She got it mostly right, but she added a lot of stuff. She said Gussie Ann drove her own car down to Georgetown to the boat dock until Bunny reminded her that nobody had cars in those days and that Gussie Ann would have been too young to drive one anyway. "Well, she had her own wagon, yeah, that's it," Big Boy said.

Bunny rolled her eyes at me. Then she grabbed my arm tight. "Oh, look at that fine child in that Camaro!" she screamed.

"Bunny, I got to go home." I started off around the steps, determined to get myself back home. This was not enough fun to get grounded for the rest of my life over.

Bam! Something grabbed me from behind and pushed me roughly against Ripley's granite wall.

"Arrrgh!" I kicked wildly, scared to death. "Lemme go!"

"Ow! Stop! It's me, girl!" Bunny yelled.

Bunny and Big Boy squashed themselves against me. "Check out that big black Lincoln," Bunny said, agitated, "going past right there!"

When I looked close at the driver of the

car, I about fainted. It was Miz Skipper! Had she seen me?

"Bet your momma told her where I was," Big Boy said rough and cussed.

"Bet she didn't have to say a thing to your grandma," I shot back. "You rode that bronco like it was your couch. I bet you sneak out down here all the time. She knew right where to find you. Now, don't you say a word about seeing me down here, you hear, Big Boy? 'Cause I didn't want to come in the first place when you asked."

"Yeah, but you're here anyway," she said, looking ugly.

I just stared hard at her until she promised. Then I waited until Miz Skipper had driven far up the street and past the bumper car rides. "Bye." I churned my toes away from the noise and lights of the Pavilion and headed for home. I didn't stop running until I hit my own street.

Sure that Momma or Daddy was going to leap out of the grass and tear me to pieces, I skittered into the back yard. I waited at the screen door for a few seconds, then tiptoed into the kitchen. Paused again. When the sink let out a gurgle, I thought I would have a heart attack. Listening hard, I sneaked into the bathroom, but the only thing I heard was Daddy snoring. After an eternity, I eased into our bedroom and got in bed, still wearing my jelly shoes, shirt, and shorts. I held my breath. All quiet.

Relieved, I went right off to sleep.

"Well, y'all, what you think?"

When I opened my left eye, I saw Hattie on her hands and knees on her bed. She wore a pair of pink leotards and a yellow and black striped bathing suit. It was Tuesday morning.

"You look like a caterpillar," giggled Maizell. "And those jokes you just told are stale on top of stale."

I opened my other eye and squinted through the bright morning sunlight at Hattie. "You'd be better off wearing regular clothes and lip-syncing, Hat," I said as nice as I could. "Do 'Telephone Man' or 'I'm a Virgin,' maybe."

"Wouldn't Momma just die!" Maizell put her hand on her hip and played like she had a microphone in her hand and sang parts of the song. "C'mon, Hat, get up and sing it with me!"

"You all ain't got no sense at all," Hattie said. "Everybody's lip-syncing, singing, or dancing. I wanna do something different. Jokes and gymnastics are the only things left for me to do that's different."

"Then do something from 'Roxanne.' That's got jokes."

"Hey, yeah!" Hattie tore off the swimsuit. "Yeah! And I could wear a pink and green plaid beret and high-top pink tennis shoes and argyles and knickers!" She ran out of the room, yelling. "Is Momma home? Momma, I got a talent! Momma, you home?"

I yawned and rolled over on my stomach. My legs were sore from all that running last night. "Maizell, now I don't know if she's gonna be better off or worse."

"At least she won't break her neck trying to do flips." Maizell poked my leg. "And you gotta get up right now or I'll tell Momma. She's gone to clean condos and said you coulda come and made some money, but you're grounded. So you gotta vacuum the house. I gotta wash the bathroom walls."

Knowing that Maizell really would tell, I dragged myself up. Trying not to let her see that I still had on my jelly shoes, I eased my feet out of the bed. Somebody down the street was playing Prince's new song that I wanted to hear up close, but I knew I wouldn't today! Grounded still!

"I'll never get off grounding," I grumbled. "Summer'll be gone, and I'll still be trunked up in this house."

"Momma says you got street feet too much. She says you sneak off when you say you're going to read in the shed, too."

My breath froze in my throat. But I tried to stay cool. I headed for the closet to get the vacuum cleaner. Did Momma know about last night? Take my soul to Jesus if she did, because my behind was going to belong to *her*.

"Momma said she didn't really think you would do that, though," Maizell went on, "because she said somebody would surely get word back to her if you were."

I took a chance. "You sound like you're talking about some ole mangy dog sleeping in the street instead of your own flesh-and-blood true sister. You and Momma don't even trust me."

"I'm just teasing you," Maizell said, looking hurt, "like you all do me."

Meanwhile, Hattie was singing her head off in time to the telephone song playing on the radio. She sounded awful, about like Big Boy yodeling. Remembering, I had to laugh out loud.

"What you laughing at?" Hattie yelled in the middle of her song. "You laughing at me?"

"No, girl. Keep on singing," I said.

After I cleaned the house I went outside and hung off the porch railing, looking for somebody to talk to. The sun burned hot, giving off the right kind of heat for a swim in the ocean or going crabbing or checking out the mall, or even just sitting down at the Pavilion. Maizell and Hattie ran past me, going to the rec center to practice in the drill team. Me, I couldn't go even to that!

I remembered the Pavilion again and had to grin. But I stopped just as quick. Here it was broad daylight and I hadn't been anywhere and hadn't seen a soul, you hear me? Everybody but me was off somewhere having fun! I got my radio out of our room and turned it on loud on the porch, just to remind everybody that I was still alive.

After a while I saw Big Head delivering newspapers. He threw Mr. Alston's newspaper high in the air as he biked past the house. The paper landed on the carport roof.

I waved at Big Head. "Can I get a paper?" I hoped he'd stop and say something, just for a minute, but I didn't want to act bold like Bunny would have.

Big Head skidded his dirt bike to a stop, spun around in a wide circle, and, kicking up sand and dirt, charged over to me. He was the best dirt-bike rider around.

"Been digging in any cemeteries lately?" he asked.

"You just wait," I said, all of a sudden mad at him for being so smart-mouth. "What do you know?"

He laughed and gave me a paper. "Good work. Maybe I'll come help you sometime. Bye."

"Good work what?"

Surprised over what he said, and feeling good that I got at least a little bit of attention, I opened the *Gumbo Grove Gazette*. I hardly ever read it. Talk about dull! Always old political stuff and nothing for kids. I glanced over the first few pages. Then my eyes hit a headline: "Alexander Morgan G. Dickson, Founder of Gumbo Grove?"

What? Right at the top of page six was this long article about Gumbo Dickson in Miz Pennyfeather's library column!

There was *my* name, too: "This week I became intrigued when Miss Raisin Stackhouse of our city inquired about a Mr. Alexander

Morgan G. Dickson," her column began. "Unfamiliar with the name, I didn't know exactly where to begin, but I found his name in the minutes of what is now our City Council. I then realized that I was about to research a fascinating bit of colorful local history that many of you might not be aware of."

I got so excited that my heart pounded and my palms got sweaty. Wait till Miss Effie saw this! Now they'd have to support her!

Miz Pennyfeather went into more detail about Gumbo Dickson: that he was mayor of Gumbo Grove from 1844 until 1850, when he died; that he owned most of Gumbo Grove and so on, like she'd told me. She ended her column with a suggestion that a monument or plaque be placed in town somewhere in his honor.

I shook the newspaper in the air like a victory flag. Needed to call Miss Effie! But how?

Little old Miz Flossie Chestnut came down the street pulling against a rope tied to her big yellow dog Bo. As usual Bo was pulling her, but not in the direction she wanted to go. She was just fussing and cussing.

"Hey, Miss Flossie," I yelled, "wanna hear something good?"

Bo dragged Miss Flossie out into the middle of the street to a McDonald's sack and began to eat the french fries scattered around it. Then he dragged her over to the dumpster. Miss Flossie was too preoccupied to bother with me.

Way up the street I saw Maizell. That gave me an idea. "Maizell!"

I jumped up and down and pointed to the paper. Of course, the first thing she wanted to know when she got there was why I was in the paper and did Momma and Daddy know?

"Oh, well, I don't know if they do or not." I sat down on the tree-stump flower bed. "You think they'll get mad? But, Maizell, I gotta get in touch with Miss Effie. C'mon and call her for me, okay?"

"If I do, I might get into it with Momma and Daddy, too, and I ain't going down that road for nobody." She chewed on her lip. Then she smiled. "But what's it worth to ya?"

"All I got is a quarter."

She got the quarter. But she also took her time going to the telephone. When she finally called, she stayed on only about five seconds.

"What'd she say?" I asked when Maizell had hung up.

"She said, 'What, baby?' and then she said, 'All right, baby.'"

"That's all?"

"You don't get much for a quarter these days."

We eyeballed each other. I dragged my jar of change out from under my bed and paid her another quarter.

"Now call her back and make sure she knows everything." I ticked them off on my fingers.

Maizell got crafty. "Maybe I should start charging by the minute. My time seems to be pretty valuable right now."

When Maizell called the second time, Miss Effie was ready. Maizell said, "Yes, ma'am," and "No, ma'am," and "I don't know" four times.

"And Raisin wants to know do you think she'll get in trouble again about talking about the cemetery?" Maizell said.

"Yes, ma'am. No, ma'am. Good-bye." Maizell hung up the telephone, smirking, with her mouth nailed shut.

"Well?"

Lips tighter than a zipper, she held out her hand and pointed to her palm.

"This is blackmail, you know." I gave her another quarter.

"Miss Effie had already seen the article, and she says to tell you she's proud of you and that whatever happens is God's will, especially if you get in trouble. And speaking of trouble, here comes Daddy, driving like he's got lead in his foot again."

I flew to our room and stuffed the newspaper in my bottom dresser drawer. Then I went into the living room. Daddy came in the back door and paused in the hallway. Gray-black mud was crusted on his legs up to his knees; some even clung to his rolled-up pants.

"Daddy, you been crabbing!" I hopped off the couch. "Did you get many?"

"Two big tubs full in the back of the truck. I'm going right out to Cypress Swamp Cove and sell 'em, soon as I clean up. You been home all day?"

When I reminded him that I was still grounded, he reminded me that he had asked me a specific question and wanted a specific answer.

"Yes, sir," I said, hurt.

"You cleaned up like you supposed to? Or you been sleeping on the couch all day?"

I told him real quiet that I had worked and stayed at home, wondering why he had to sound so mean. Maybe he had already heard about the article.

"Then you can come help me sell these crabs," he said. He put a little smile on his face. "You gotta get off grounding and help me out. Need ya, girl!" He went into the bathroom.

I about jumped ten feet into the air. Maybe he wasn't mad at me after all! I ran out to the kitchen and grabbed the clipboard off its hook, then rummaged in the drawer for our special crabbing pen.

When we went out selling crabs, I kept track of all the ones sold and made change. Because customers sometimes forgot to bring a pot to put the crabs in, I kept a supply of sacks in the shed. I got an armful out of the shed, but before I left, I glanced over at the shelf where I had hidden the record books. My heart stopped. They were gone!

Dropping the sacks, I clambered up on the chair and patted around on the shelf. Where were they? Who had them? Momma? Poppa? Hattie? Maizell? Did someone come in and steal them?

"You coming or not?" Daddy hollered.

I picked up the sacks and, trying to hide my troubled face, went out to the truck.

When I climbed up into the back of the truck, cracklings and rustlings rose from the tubs. Dozens of bronze, blue, and yellow pincers waved in the air. With a long pair of tongs, I carefully reached into the tub and, clasping a pincer, lifted out a beady-eyed, wriggling brown crab.

Gently I set it in an empty tub where it skittered sideways away from me, claws raised like a boxer's fists.

"You're gonna taste fine to somebody real soon," I told it. By moving the crabs from a full tub like this one to an empty one, I was able to count them quicker. We had nine dozen. At $3.50 a dozen, we could make close to $32.00. If they sold fast, we'd be through in a couple hours. The customers picked the ones they wanted. If we had only small ones left, we'd drop the price to $2.50 a dozen. Some folks liked to buy a whole bushel basket of crabs, but Daddy wouldn't sell them that way. He said you would make more selling a couple dozen at a time. The bait Daddy used to catch them with—chicken necks and flounder heads— was free, so we didn't worry about what you called overhead to subtract from our profit.

Daddy handed me a sprinkler can of creek water, which I sprinkled over the crabs to keep them cool and alive. Then I covered the tubs with wet pieces of burlap. Daddy started up the truck, and we headed for Cypress Swamp Cove. I sat in the back with the crabs, my chin on my arms. A thought hit me. Maybe Daddy knew about the record books and had me trapped back here. Maybe he was going to give me a really hard talking-to once he got me away from the house. No, I shook that out of my head. Daddy wasn't like that. He liked to holler and shout, but he wasn't nasty.

But then I heard Bunny's voice inside my head right then. "Forget the books! Ole cemetery stuff! You out the house and out the yard, girl! Go for it!"

All of a sudden the street was alive and busy. People!

Reverend Walker drove by in his Buick and waved at me. I saw Lucinda and Timika Bellamy ride their bicycles across the school yard up the street. And over there, wearing their burgundy robes, the New Africa Senior Choir stood on the church steps while Mr. Zack the photographer took a picture of them. When Daddy honked, Mr. Zack turned around and waved. He and his wife, who was a writer, had a business called Positive Images, and they went all over everywhere taking pictures and writing stories. They came to our pageant, too. Almost everybody else waved. Miz Aussie Skipper was there, but she didn't wave. She just stared at me like she could see straight into my brains.

We bumped over the Fifteenth Street drainage ditch bridge toward Lebo's Barber

Shop, Lebo's Food Mart, and Lebo's Blue Flame Café and Bar. Bunches of guys drinking out of paper sacks leaned against the walls of the Blue Flame. A few of them played cards on the front porch of the grocery. Girls in tight shorts and T-shirts cut off above the belly button leaned into the windows of cars parked every which way in the sandy parking lot. Music thumped everywhere.

A guy grinned at me and winked. Embarrassed and flattered and scared, I slid down into the truck. That was how I felt each time I went past Lebo's corner. People shopped in Mr. Lebo's stores, but it was mainly a hangout where anybody—kids, tourists, anybody—could buy marijuana, cocaine, and everything else, right out in the open. The police wouldn't do anything because it was outside city limits. Daddy acted like he couldn't stand the place. If we girls were with him and he was out selling vegetables or crabs, like now, he wouldn't stop down here. He'd take us home first and then come back. He'd skin me alive and turn it into a belt if he caught me anywhere near Mr. Lebo's or even heard of me being down here. I wouldn't want to go, though.

"Hey, check them crabs!" Daddy hollered.

I scrambled over to the tubs. Dozens of pincers flew up in the air again when I lifted the burlap, and crabs clumped on top of each other, trying to pull themselves up to the top of the tubs. But the other crabs would pull them back down. Reverend Walker gave us a sermon about crabs in a barrel once. He said that's how some Black folks were. Didn't want anybody else to move up the ladder and out of the barrel, trying to pull them back down into the barrel with the rest of them. Each time I saw them pull each other back down, I thought about that. When I sprinkled more water over them and got them cool and comfortable, they settled back down. And I thought about that, too.

"I know that Lebo pays the police to keep them quiet and not arrest those drug pushers," Daddy hollered out the window at me like he always did when we went past. "You stay away from there, you hear? It's a den of sin and a blemish to the community! Somebody ought to close him down!"

"Well, how come the church or nobody ever told Mr. Lebo to get rid of all the dope pushers?" I yelled back. I usually said the same thing, too.

" 'Cause it ain't the church's job," Daddy said, just like I knew he would. "That's the police's and the city's job. This whole corner is corrupting you young people worse and worse."

But why did Daddy go to the Blue Flame to buy beer on Sundays, when it was illegal to buy it, and to play pool when the bar was supposed to be closed? Seemed like he wouldn't want to be down there, either, getting corrupted. But I kept that part to myself.

Soon Cypress Swamp Cove's gray brick pillars loomed in front of us. Daddy pulled up to Mr. Bellamy's tiny security guard office and handed him his driver's license and his pass. I never knew why Daddy still had to do that after all the years he'd been coming in and out of here, but he did. He and Mr. Bellamy cracked a couple of jokes. Then Mr. Bellamy said Daddy could go on through.

Cypress Swamp Cove was a fancy golf course with condominiums, villas, and a dozen huge houses dotting the green. Long, slender blades of pampas grass on both sides of the lane gently waved in the wind. This was a very expensive place to live, I knew. I hadn't ever seen any of our folks look like they lived here, but Daddy said a few Black folks from Virginia and Georgia vacationed in their condos here. A couple of joggers hopped along a neat trail behind a colony of gray wood villas. In front of each house was a perfect square of neatly trimmed, lush green grass. Mercedes and Porsches sat in their monogrammed garages.

I wondered what it would be like to live inside a golf course. Must be what some folks really wanted to do so bad that they were willing to spend a whole lot of money to do it. I knew a couple of girls from school who lived in here. Sometimes they spoke, and sometimes they didn't.

Jennifer Crowley told me she was always afraid that some golfer would knock a golf ball through her dining room window and into her plate. Jennifer was nice. Sometimes we ate lunch together, and we chose up on the same side when we played volleyball or baseball in gym.

There was Jennifer right there, standing on the tennis court with a Frisbee and her poodle Mitzy. When she saw our truck, she waved and started to run across the tennis court. Daddy drove on out to the houses. We stopped at the first few, and Daddy walked to the side door with a sack containing three big crabs. Nobody was home at any of them, though.

When we got to Jennifer's house, she had already gotten back home. She came out with her father, a big blond-haired man wearing a tennis shirt and shorts. In a few minutes he came back out carrying an ice chest. He wanted two dozen.

"Gimme that one and that one and that one," the man said, pointing so fast I could hardly keep up. I picked up a big blue-clawed crab with my tongs and started to put it in his ice chest.

"No, not that one, you dummy, that one! It's bigger!" the man said.

I looked at Daddy, and Daddy looked at the man.

"He calls everybody dummy," Jennifer said. "He calls me dummy, too."

I still didn't like what he said. He handed me a five dollar bill. When I hesitated, waiting for more money, he said, "Two fifty a dozen, right?"

"Three fifty," Daddy told him.

The man slammed down the chest. "I'm not gonna pay three fifty for those things. That's highway robbery. Two fifty or you can take 'em back."

Daddy and the man stared at each other. Jennifer's face turned red. She looked at me and then looked away. I wanted to snatch our crabs out of that nasty man's hands and bawl him out. But I also felt sorry for Jennifer, because I knew her father's rudeness wasn't her fault.

"Well, Raisin! That you? Do you have some crabs?"

I turned around. It was Jennifer's mother, riding up the bike trail toward us on her bicycle. She peered into the ice chest. "That's a fine crop of crabs. Two dozen, hunh? How much are they?"

"Three fifty a dozen," said Jennifer, "but Daddy says they cost too much. He called Raisin a dummy, like he does me."

Her mother patted me on the arm. "Daddy shouldn't call names. Ellis," she told the man, "this is Raisin Stackhouse. She was in the newspaper today. She's a celebrity. She and Jennifer are in the same class. Good job, Raisin!"

Jennifer's father thinned his lips at me like he wanted to smile but couldn't.

"Have you been paid, Raisin?" When I shook my head, Mrs. Crowley reached into her purse and paid me. Then she jerked her head at Jennifer and the man. "Let's go, gang. We've got some crab cooking to do, right?"

I got in the cab of the truck with Daddy and we drove off. "That Ellis always was a nasty, tight-fisted something," Daddy said. "He didn't remember me, but I sure remember him. His momma was always decent, though, but his daddy was a humdinger. Baby, you sure Lord ain't nobody's dummy. And I was gonna let him know that, too."

I didn't say anything, but he made me feel

good inside for wanting to take up for me. I wish he had said something, though.

"Celebrity, hunh?"

"Oh, no," I said quickly.

"What's this about your name in the paper?"

"Nothing."

"Then you saw the paper?"

Oh-oh, here it comes. "Kinda."

"What was it you *kinda* saw giving your name in the paper but yet and still it didn't say nothing about you?"

"About some man who founded Gumbo Grove," I said.

"And how'd your name get in the paper in connection with it?"

"Well, it was in Miz Pennyfeather's library column, and we had kinda talked about this man, but that's all I did, Daddy, I swear to Jesus. I haven't been near that ole cemetery or Miss Effie or nobody. And Miz Pennyfeather just took it on herself to write about him, honest."

"How'd you know about this man to talk about him?"

"I just wanted to know," I whispered, miserable.

"Raisin!"

"Miss Effie told me to look him up."

"Miss Effie!" He turned his head around so he could stare at me full face for a hard second.

I opened my mouth, but nothing came out at first. And then the words came flying. " 'Cause I didn't know who founded Gumbo Grove. I mean, Miss Effie said he was buried in—I mean, the record books—"

"And what'd we tell you about Miss Effie?" He jerked the truck to a stop and shook his finger in my face. "Hunh? What record books? Girl, I oughta—"

"Oh, Lenwood, you came just at the right time!"

A red-haired woman in blue jeans called to him from across the street. "Hope you've got some crabs in there!"

Talk about right on time!

"Oh, Lenwood, I've had steamed crabs on my mind all morning," the woman said, coming to the truck as we got out. "Give me three dozen."

"You don't remember me, but I know who you are," she said to me. "I'm Miz Pennyfeather's niece. She told me about you. She's coming over to have dinner with us tonight. You're a smart young lady. And, Lenwood, you must be very proud of her."

Daddy looked at me and then at the

woman. "Why, yes, I am," he said. "I surely am. People need to know that. They—" he stopped when he saw I was staring at him. "Well, you let me know when you want some more crabs, and I'll be around directly."

9

Daddy didn't say anything else, which was a relief. Now if only he would just *stay* quiet until we finished our rounds and got back home.

So far, so good. He kept quiet. Relieved, I finally relaxed and began to stare at the rows of condos along Cypress Swamp Road and daydream that I was driving into Hilton Head. We pulled up to our house, I in the driver's seat of my red Trans Am.

"Raisin!" Daddy's voice woke me from my daydream.

I froze against the door.

"How is it you got hold of the record books is what I want to know."

I took a deep breath. "Well, it's like this, see. Miss Effie, see, she—"

"All this cemetery stuff! That's at the bottom of it, isn't it? All this Gumbo Dickson stuff! You ain't even been on earth long enough to have any kinda idea what opening up this mess is liable to do bad!"

"Like what?"

"Like make things awful, the way it was before! Our folks haven't always had it good around here like we do now. Used to be a shame. We had to work for nickels and dimes, live in shacks about to fall down on our heads every time it rained and the wind blew. Puttin' pans on the bed so the bed wouldn't get soaked. Now we got better jobs and halfway decent houses, can uplift ourselves, try to keep off so much welfare!"

I wanted to roll my eyes. I'd heard this same story over and over. I couldn't understand why he was so upset. Miss Effie got upset the same way. Things were different now, weren't they? Why be so bothered over what happened way back when? Seemed like everybody could just take it in stride and maybe laugh about it, I thought to myself.

"But you're dragging up stuff nobody wants to hear about," Daddy said.

"Nobody who, Daddy? I do."

"Who? You?" He looked at me like I was crazy. "I'm talking about certain White folks around here want to get all the credit for everything done, that's who. Certain Colored, too. And there you go again, opening up old sores. Sores, I'm talking about. Tell them about all these things we done here. Them White folks'll wake up quick and snatch away everything we got, just like they did that Dickson fella. And be Colored folks helping them to do it!"

"Like Miz Skipper, Daddy?"

"Girl, you got a mouth on you won't quit!"

I slumped against the door, afraid to say anything. But I had to. "But, Daddy, Miz Pennyfeather hasn't been mean, and she's White. And Jennifer's mother wasn't mean, and she's White."

"Unh-hunh, but you forgot Jennifer's daddy, didn't you? And as for Miz Pennyfeather, she probably don't know Dickson was Black."

I sat up straight. "So he was, really?" Well, what did I say that for? Daddy got to denying he had said anything about Mr. Dickson being Black. So I left that part alone. I went back to Miz Pennyfeather. "What if Miz Pennyfeather knows all about him, Daddy? What if she does know? Didn't seem to make any difference to her."

He frowned at me hard, and his eyes kinda bugged out like they do when he's thinking hard and is mad at the same time. "Just what makes you think she *does* know? Weren't you supposed to be grounded and not go nowhere, not even the library?"

"I ain't been out the yard, Daddy, to go to nobody's library, I swear. But, Daddy, Miz Pennyfeather can look up history better than almost anybody else around here. So maybe she does know, but it hasn't stopped her."

Daddy got out and slammed shut the door. "Get your behind in the house and keep your mouth shut," he said. "Don't you say nothing about me and Gumbo Dickson." Well, I opened my big mouth again, I told myself, feeling miserable. I'll be eighty years old and still grounded.

"Miss Effie called," Momma said when I came into the house, "to tell you they're going to elect new officers Thursday night. She said everybody in the church must have seen that story"—Momma pinned me to the wall with her eyeballing—"and now they're yap, yap about Gumbo this and Gumbo that buried in our cemetery. Or did you already know?"

Talk about a loaded question!

"Well, if she didn't, she does now," Daddy said. "You and Raisin's just alike: talk too much and ask too many questions."

"Raisin," said Momma, ignoring Daddy, "please keep on working with Hattie about her attitude and the pageant. She's doing better but, well, you know. It's on Saturday. This is Tuesday. You got four days to get the kinks out of her. Hattie's been practicing, I'll give her that. Maizell's helping hard, too. I know that telephone song by heart now myself. Oh, and she's got rehearsal Thursday night. You go with her, hear, 'cause I got to go to that church meeting. And Miss Effie told me about you having the record books."

"Maybe if you help your sister more you'd stay out of other people's business," Daddy said. "Miss Effie didn't need to hand those books over to you. But I got them now."

First I was relieved; the books were safe. But what he just said hurt. He made it sound like I had asked to borrow them. What would he do if I told Momma that he was the one told me Gumbo Dickson was a Black man? That was information he was so busy trying to cover up from my knowing in the first place! I stopped to think about it. Daddy never liked what Grandma Stackhouse talked about, either, and I'd heard she was a humdinger during the fifties, sixties, and seventies, marching and boycotting!

I put the most honest expression on my face that I could and looked Daddy square in the eye. "Momma, can I go over to Bunny's, please? I've been good for over a week! I was real good with Daddy, and didn't talk hardly at all about Gumbo Dickson or the cemetery, did I, Daddy?" I looked up at him, big-eyed and innocent. "Only thing I know about him is what I read in the paper, ain't that right, Daddy?"

Daddy stared back at me. Then he cleared his throat, shrugged, and turned his head away. "Yeah, she did all right. Just asks too many daggone questions." Then he looked back at me. I saw something like respect in his eyes. Was that what it was?

"Well, then, if you say so, Lenwood, 'cause I got to go along with what you say," Momma said. She turned to me. "It doesn't sound like this is your fault." "Maybe Bunny can tell you what to do with Hattie. Don't be gone long, else you'll be right back here, nose flat on screen, watching the world go by. I guess you're off grounding for now, though."

Before she could add to that, I flew out of the house and into the street. I felt so free I had to jump up and down once, spin around and do a short moonwalk.

"Lookit that crazy thing!"

"Who got the music, Raisin?"

Embarrassed, I walked civilized past Mandy and Marvadean sitting on Mandy's front porch, like I didn't know what a moonwalk was.

"Shake it, sugar!" Marvadean shrieked.

"Your momma shake it!" I yelled back. Right then Mandy's mother walked into the front yard. She looked at me strangely.

I about died, right? But kept on stepping.

Bunny was getting ready to leave when I got over to her house. "I saw your name in the paper." She braided Candy's hair on the front porch. Candy squirmed and screeched. "You are big-time now, and I'm scared of you! I was gonna ask did you want to come long with me to Miz Mubarak's Thrift Shop, but you too high-class now!"

"Oh, girl, quit!" I laughed, loving it, glad to be with her again.

She stopped braiding long enough to throw an arm around my neck and hug me. "You do like you say you're gonna do, don't you? Girl, you're all right, even though you're just as crazy as a loon."

Candy jerked away, but Bunny pulled her back. "One more braid, honey. Raisin," and she plopped back on the step with Candy's head between her knees, "I'm gonna tell you what happens next. They gonna turn that old graveyard into Disneyland, except call it Grave-yard Land and charge five dollars for people to get in and get thrilled to death. With Michael Jackson look-alikes."

"You're awful! Hey, I'm not grounded anymore!"

"About time, too. So do you wanna go to the thrift shop? These kids need some under-wear and some more T-shirts! Momma gave me ten dollars."

I told her that going to the thrift shop was not real high on my list right now, since I'd just got out of jail, right? "But I'll see you when you get back."

Over at the Gumbo Limbo Sin-Sin stood outside announcing news to Junebug. They said "Hey" when I came up and told me they'd heard about the story. That got me puffed with pride for a hot moment.

But then Junebug cut me right back down. "Daddy said you're a gossip bad as an old woman. And then he said the cat was out the bag now because of you and that someone oughta put a lock on your mouth, and—"

"Oughta put one on yours, too," Sin-Sin told him, looking at me. "Raisin, is that slave girl you told us about in this same cemetery?"

I smiled a little, glad she'd asked me something that I felt good about. But I just said, "Yeah."

"Deidra says she's gonna kick everybody's behind getting the most ads for the pageant," Sin-Sin said. "She's been bragging and bragging. I bet she's gonna beat everybody easy. Beat Hattie first."

"Deidra's just talking." I looked at the sky like it was the most important thing in my life. Mr. Easau came out just then and sat under the awning.

"Deidra's gonna sing 'My Emotion,' " Sin-Sin said. "She's got her sportswear picked out. Everything's lavender. But she's going blue and white in formal wear—open-toe sky-blue sandals with a pump heel, pale blue stockings, and a powder-blue silk sash to complement. Miss Erma's gonna pile her hair on top of her head and let side curls hang down in front of each ear. And blue ribbons and lavender flowers as barretts."

"Daggone, you've been spying hard; you're

an ole gossip worse'n Raisin." Junebug looked sympathetic at me. "Hattie might as well drop out now and save your folks some clothes money."

"Hattie's gonna do all right, okay?" I said loud, frowning. "Okay? Okay?"

"C'mere, baby," Mr. Easau said to me.

I went over, stood polite, and waited, my face hot, wondering what he wanted to talk about. The article? Did he know about the record books? Had he seen me at the Pavilion that night? He thought I couldn't take talk about Hattie?

"You see, not everybody's gonna tell ya what's good for ya, but I am." He squinted at me, spit some tobacco, and leaned back. "You done good when you asked questions about that Gumbo Dickson. About time! But you're gonna have to do a whole lot more to make people move and get them to do. So you keep asking questions. You'll get them to do. Do something, for sure!"

He talked to me like that for a good ten minutes. Then he rambled off into something about the devil. But what he said about me made me feel good. So I said thank you and looked around for my friends. Junebug and Sin-Sin were gone, but I saw Big Head on the other side of the street delivering the *Charleston*

Chronicle Black newspaper. When he spied me, he swung around, rode closer, and threw one at me. I caught it with no problem. I liked to read it. Sometimes Momma or Daddy got the *Pee Dee Observer*, too. Both papers were full of history, but hardly anything about Calvary County.

"I know who Gumbo Dickson is, too," he said.

" 'Cause you read it in the paper, Big Head."

" 'Cause I looked him up in an old book. It's even got a little bitty picture of him." He pedaled off.

Why hadn't I thought about looking him up myself? I have history books at home. I ran through a cloud of dust after him. "Big Head, where can I get that book?"

"My uncle in Columbia has a copy."

My shoulders sagged. "Columbia might as well be a million miles away." I wished I hadn't told the Lord that I didn't care to go to Columbia.

"But he let me hold it last year, and I'm still holding it," he added. He put a solemn look on his face. "If you wanna see it, you gotta promise not to call me Big Head anymore."

"It was just a name. I didn't mean it." I felt ashamed, and promised.

"I gotta finish up my route first," he said. "I'll meet you at the Limbo in about an hour, okay?"

I hurried home and thumbed through my history books. Nothing! Then I jumped on my bike and hustled back to the Limbo. There was Big Head—I mean Jeff—showing the book to Junebug and Sin-Sin. He was right: the book was old. Its pages were brown with age, and it had a fancy illustration of a big red rose growing around the shape of Africa on its cover. Curly writing was everywhere. GREAT AFRO-AMERICAN HEROES was written on the front.

We watched Jeff flip through the pages. "Anything ugly in there?" Junebug asked.

"No, he's looking for this man," Sin-Sin informed him, "who found Gumbo Grove."

"Where'd he find it?"

Sin-Sin pointed to the ground. "Right here."

"Here!" Jeff jabbed at the book. I leaned in hard and saw a picture of a man with a thin nose, long beard, and stern eyes looking back at me from the page. "Here, Raisin, here he is."

My eyes dashed over the words beneath his picture. "Birthdate circa 1790; Alexander Morgan Grove ("Gumbo") Dickson. War of 1812 hero; politician; merchant. Best known for heroism during Chesapeake Campaign in 1814 when British and American troops fought in Washington, D.C.; founder of Gumbo Grove, South Carolina; state senator from District 14; first term, 1830; served two terms; married Veranda Dozier Watson 1825. Died 1850."

"State senator!"

"I've heard of that war."

"So what, Big Head?" said Junebug. "He's just an ole ugly man."

"I think this is very important, because it proves Gumbo Dickson was a Black man and did big things!" I cut my eyes at Junebug. "And don't call him Big Head anymore. His name is Jeff."

Everybody went "ohhh!" at that. Jeff's ears turned red. Mr. Easau got up from his chair and came over to us.

"What you kids got now?" he asked, eyeing the book. Jeff handed it to him. "I heard something about this fella from way back," he said when he had finished reading. "It got clean buried in my brain. Things that get handed down do tend to stick in your mind, though. I heard about one of ours being mayor or something here one time, but there was so much stink about it that don't nobody talk much about it now. Why you all reading about him?"

Everybody pointed to me. Mr. Easau said, "Unh-hunh." He sat back down. "Just after he died was when the stuff came down bad."

"Bad how?" Jeff asked.

"This is what I heard, but you can't put anything to it. Gumbo Dickson owned 'most all this town and more. He was supposed to have been a big senator, too. That's right. He died a rich man, they say. They buried him in Memorial Cemetery way up the road here. Well, he left a will. That will said, 'Being of sound mind and of African descent.' "

"What's that mean?" Junebug asked.

"Everybody thought Gumbo Dickson was White, see. Could you tell he was a Negro from looking at that picture? No, indeed. See, the White people felt he had betrayed them by not saying he was part Colored, looking like that and doing what he did and not really be all White. Remember these were still slavery days. They didn't have any free Black people up around here! Anybody free who came here didn't stop."

Mr. Easau handed the book back to Jeff. "They dug his grave up out of Memorial

Cemetery, the White cemetery, because they said he didn't belong there. His wife was Colored, too. They made her sell most of her land. They did let her keep a good bit on the edge of town where he had built their home and had their farm. She set some of that land aside and had him buried there. She was, too, so they say. Little by little, other Colored started to bury there, a few folks even had their slaves buried there."

"Do you think he had slaves, too?" Jeff asked.

Mr. Easau laughed. "Boy, you can sure ask some questions! I don't know!" He clasped his hands behind his head, smiling broadly, then spitting tobacco. "You younguns made me remember things I'd forgot was there! This stuff was told to me back when I was in school."

We all went "ohhh," because Mr. Easau was old, old. So it had to have been a long, long time ago.

"Anyway, when the war came along through here, the Civil War, the Dickson house was burned down."

"Is Gussie Ann Vereen, that little slave girl, buried in the same cemetery? Is it New Africa's, like Miss Effie said?" I was really excited now.

"I don't know nothing about a slave girl

named Gussie," Mr. Easau chuckled. "And some folks'll tell you not to believe that story about Gumbo Dickson. And I don't know where he's buried. There's cemeteries all over this county, and there's a bunch more that's been here and gone forever. He could be in any of them, or none, far as I'm concerned."

"But Miss Effie said—"

"Oh, girl, there you go again," said Sin-Sin.

A light went on inside my head. "Thanks, Mr. Easau. I gotta go!"

When I broke into a run for home, Jeff pedaled after me. "You've gotta get maps of the cemeteries if you're gonna try and find his grave, right?"

I slowed down. "You got maps, too?"

"No. Do you?"

I grinned. "Maybe!"

When I got home, Daddy was sitting in his armchair looking at the record books. I eased into the room and sat down on the couch, bracing myself for another bawling-out. When he didn't say anything, but kept on reading, I perched on the arm of his chair beside him and read along, too.

After a while he spoke. "This has got a lot that I never even knew. Stuff nobody in the church even talks about anymore!" He looked up at me with one eyebrow cocked high. "They had people went to college and got degrees way back in the 1920s. Talk about how this person was a cook for such-and-such and how well they cooked. Talk about how that fella was a brick mason and where he built houses. Farmers knowing how to grow crops. And none of us on welfare." He closed the book. "Have you read through both these books?"

"No, but I'd sure like to. Daddy, Jeff's got a book that tells about Gumbo Dickson and what he done, and Mr. Easau said he'd heard of him, too." I put a plea in my voice, knowing I was taking a big chance of being grounded again.

"Daddy, this is the biggest hero I have ever heard of in my life, and they say he's buried right in our own county, and maybe in that old cemetery! That book Jeff has said he was a state senator, too! Daddy, can I please look in the record books and see if there's a map showing where he's supposed to be buried? Please?"

Daddy stared at me until I thought he'd burn a hole in my brain. Boy, here it comes now, I told myself, and shrank back a little. When he saw me do that, he put a soft look in his eyes and smiled. He patted me on my arm with his finger, then tapped the record book.

"You know, I'd clean forgot all the kin I had buried in there. Like great Uncle Ezekial," he said quietly. "That fella showed me how to crab, how to swim in a river, and how to swim in the ocean. There's a difference, you know. And Step-grandaddy Sye McCray. I climbed up in a sweet gum tree the day he died." He sighed. "And cried till the sun went down. I was nine years old."

Daddy looked at me with sadness in his face. "Sometimes it's better to forget."

"Why?"

"So you don't have to remember the pain. A lotta people won't think about the dead because they went through so much pain when they had to put them in those graves in the first place. Some folks get down sick for years in bed and can't do for themselves, and just waste away. That hurts when you have to see it and can't do nothing about it. We didn't have any doctors around, no hospitals, no nothing. Nothing for us. You put stuff away in your mind."

I never thought about Daddy being a little boy and crying. I always thought of him being Daddy and hollering. I knew, though, if I thought hard enough about him that I'd want to cry, too. "I don't want to make people feel bad, Daddy. Am I doing that with this cemetery stuff? And Miss Aussie, too?"

Momma came in and looked at us. We didn't say anything for a minute. "Well, Raisin, I might as well tell you. Most of us knew that man was buried back in the cemetery. But nobody wanted to talk about him because of what happened. But he's listed right in the maps in the record book. So now I guess everybody's gonna find out all kinds of things about each other."

That made me feel even worse. "But maybe we better not say where he is," I said, miserable.

"Corinne," Daddy said to Momma, "can you recollect somebody named Connell God-bolt who was a mason and laid brick for the steps of City Hall?"

"Yes, he was your cousin on your father's side."

"I knew he was kin, but I didn't know he did the steps. I been up and down those steps all these years and never once knew. Why don't they tell us these things?"

"Because Miz Skipper didn't want anybody to know, I bet," I said.

"I been reading and reading these record books," Daddy said. "There are some really famous people for around here. The history of New Africa's cemetery is really the history of us here in Gumbo Grove and Calvary County, isn't it? That's what you been trying to tell me, Raisin?"

"Yes! But Miss Effie said Miss Aussie didn't want anybody to read the books because of the stuff in there about her relatives being slaves and prisoners. That's why she wants to be secretary, so she can erase all the stuff she doesn't like."

"Raisin, you're gossiping," said Momma.

"She said Miss Aussie wouldn't let her say much to anybody about the history, not even when the church had Men's Day and Women's Day. She said just to stick to the money part. She—"

"You sure got to be grown quick, getting into grown folks' business," Daddy said. "Your momma said to stop gossiping."

I hung my head, frustrated and confused at both of them. They could understand on one hand but not on the other!

"What's the church going to do, and does anybody care?" Daddy said to Momma.

"I can think of three who do," she said. "Raisin, Miss Effie, and me."

My mouth fell open. "Care about what? The cemetery? You *do*?"

"I've been caring for a long time, but especially ever since I listened to your tape about Uncle Sarvis," she said. "The least I can do is go clean off his grave. He sure was nice to me."

"I feel that way about Connell Godbolt," Daddy said. "People ought to know more about the things we did in this town. We ought to be more proud of the good than worried about the bad, I swear." Daddy got to hollering. "Nobody better do me like they did Sarvis and his fish business. Why, my cousin helped to build that City Hall!"

"Lower your voice, Lenwood," Momma said.

"Humph! Raisin, you got three who care? Make me number four!"

I began to grin so hard I thought my face would break. I bent over to hug him, but he ducked his head and pretended to straighten out the cover of the record book. So I just pecked him on the cheek, and then he grinned hard, too.

10

The next morning Hattie burst outside to where I was on the front porch. She looked like she was about to break open from some secret I could tell she had blown up inside her.

"How're you coming with the pageant?" I asked. "Can I help?"

"I got my dress picked out, and nobody but me knows what it looks like," she said proudly.

"Shoot, I want to see it. Hey, don't you think you ought to tell Momma so she can check it for color and size and price and stuff?"

"It fits; I tried it on. It doesn't cost much, either. But you keep quiet!" She got fierce;

then she burst out laughing and went back inside.

That meant Hattie wanted me to tell Momma she had her dress picked out. "What did you just tell Raisin?" I heard Momma say from inside. Well, no worry about Momma not knowing now! I hurried into the house after Hattie, but she ran into the bathroom and locked the door.

Momma charged to the bathroom door and rattled the knob. "You should have told me a long time ago you had a dress picked out. Hattie, open this door!" She banged on it with her fist. "I don't want no foolishness out of you. If you want a dress, you better get to gettin' so I can go look at it."

"It's liable to be gone by now, anyway," Maizell said.

"No, 'cause I put a five dollar deposit on it," Hattie said through the door.

We all raised our eyebrows at each other. "So what does it look like?" Momma asked her through the door.

"It's a secret."

"If you don't come outta there this minute so we can get to gettin', you *ain't* gettin'!" Momma declared. We giggled. She winked at us.

"One, two—"

Hattie flew out like the toilet had over-flowed. "It's at Sophisticated Girls, and it's on sale for sixty-nine dollars plus tax. Is that too much? Please, you gotta get it. It's so fine!"

"Tell me why you have to be so secretive about everything," Momma said to Hattie. There was relief on Momma's face. "The pageant's practically on top of us, and I'm worried about what all I got to get for you, and you've already picked out your dress."

Momma broke out into a smile and shook her head. "Hattie, I swear, you are something. Now, c'mon, let's get to gettin'!"

So we all went hurrying out into the steamy morning and sweated half to death fast-walking up the street, dodging traffic as we raced across the highway and over to the mall. Hattie hopped into Sophisticated Girls like she owned it. She pulled a piece of paper out of her shorts pocket and said something to the woman standing by a clothes rack.

"Okay, Hattie," the woman said, and turning to another rack pulled out a paper garment bag and handed it to her.

"Don't anybody come in," Hattie warned as she went into the dressing room.

"I hope it doesn't look like something from *Hee Haw*," Maizell whispered. "You know how she likes to sit and watch that show."

"Shh, she's coming out. Oh, look at you!"

Hattie stood before us in a soft pink ruffled, sleeveless chiffon dress. It had a layered skirt trimmed with thin black lace. The skirts stuck out stiffly around her legs.

"Aren't you pretty!" Momma clapped her hands to her face and walked all the way around Hattie. "And you picked this out yourself? You look so dainty!"

We walked around her, staring and admiring. I suddenly felt shy, like I was seeing a new Hattie I hadn't seen since Easter. And even Maizell was pleased.

"But you can't wear jelly shoes with that dress," Momma said. We all laughed, Hattie, too. Momma let her pick out some matching hair combs and paid the clerk.

We walked out of the store, congratulating Hattie, and headed for the shoe store. Sin-Sin ran up to me, got the latest on Hattie's dress, then dragged me off to behind the water fountain. "Girl, everybody's looking for you!"

"Everybody who?"

"Daddy got a call from Miz Aussie Skipper who got a call from Miz Pennyfeather who got a call from Channel Sixty-six TV. They want to do a story on Gumbo Dickson. They want to know where he's buried!"

"So?"

"Well, from the way Daddy was saying, 'Calm down,' Miz Skipper musta been some upset. Miz Pennyfeather called Miz Skipper, see."

"What's that got to do with people looking for me?"

"I can keep a secret, Raisin; I already know." Sin-Sin looked pleased with herself. "Daddy called Miss Effie to get her to look in some record books, and Miss Effie said you had them. Is this the book Big Head—I mean, Jeff—had?"

I shook my head and told her it was the church records.

Her eyes narrowed. "What're you doing with them? Oh, you're in trouble now! Especially because Miss Aussie knows you've got them. She might make you give them back."

I sat down on a bench and stared at the water gushing up from the plastic oyster shell in the middle of the water fountain.

"What're you gonna do?" Sin-Sin asked.

"Tell Momma is all I can think of." When I stood up and looked around, I saw Maizell. I told her I was going home and to tell Momma.

"Lordie, let's get out of here before Miss Aussie shows up here, too!" I shot out for the door, and Sin-Sin followed.

"When you get home, I bet she's gonna

be sitting on your doorstep," Sin-Sin said as we trotted across the boulevard. Hot air rushed by as we dodged cars. "You're gonna have to sneak into your own house."

We trotted home through the chaos of RVs, cars, tourists, and mopeds. When we got to my street, we ducked quick behind Mr. Green's oleander bushes. When I looked back, I saw turning onto our street Miss Aussie's big black Lincoln.

"Sin-Sin, you go on to my house and act like you're looking for me, okay? I'ma sneak in through the back and look in the record books for the cemetery map."

"What if she wants to know if I've seen you? What'll I say?"

"Stall her. You know we don't lock the doors; she can just walk right in, get the record books, and split. I gotta get the doors locked! Say anything! You know how to talk any other time!"

"I'm a preacher's kid," Sin-Sin protested. "I can't tell lies."

I rolled my eyes and peered through the bushes. "You told one just then. If you see Junebug, Jeff, or Bunny, tell them to meet us at the cemetery in half an hour so we can find the grave. I gotta go!"

"Us? But I don't want to go to a cemetery!"

I was already running through the back yards. When I reached my own, I slipped along our hedges to the kitchen door, carefully opened it, locked it, and then edged into the living room. The record books sat in plain sight on the table in front of the living room window.

I hoped Miz Skipper hadn't already seen them. Or seen me, either! Crawling on my hands and knees to the front door, I quickly reached up and locked it. Whew! Then I crawled to the table and cautiously slid the first book down. Squinched under the table, I turned quickly to the back. The maps! On the opposite page was a numbered list of names of people. Number one was Alexander Morgan G. Dickson. I traced my finger over the name, like I was seeing it for the first time. Then I searched the map for number one. There it was, smack dab in the middle of the cemetery.

When the doorbell rang, I about croaked! If I moved, whoever was at the door would see me. All they had to do was lean a little and look through the window! It rang again and again. Had to be Miss Aussie! Then she began to bang on the door. Talk about sweat running down somebody's face! If she saw me, I knew I'd have to go to the door.

"Raisin, open up!"

Sin-Sin! I hurried to the door. "I hope

you found the map," she said, coming in. "That ole pinch-nose woman grilled me about where you were like she thought I was her spy. She said you ain't got any business with those books. She said she's called a meeting Thursday night at the church to get this matter straightened out. That's what she said."

"I already know about the meeting," I said. "It's for the election."

"It could be about the cemetery, too. Daddy says Miss Aussie can double-cross what meetings are about. I heard him tell Momma that he could walk in the door of the church for one meeting and come out having been in another."

I snapped my fingers. "And Hattie's rehearsal's Thursday night. Well, she's not gonna get these books any time soon if I can help it." I grabbed them up, ran into our room, and after closing the door, snatched off a pillowcase and slid them inside. Then I pushed them way under my bed. And then I called Jeff, Junebug, and Bunny. Bunny was home. She said she'd look for Jeff and Junebug.

"C'mon, Raisin, I gotta get back home," Sin-Sin called. "And I don't want to go to no cemetery!"

I got on my bike, and she hopped on

behind. We zigzagged along the street, watching out for Miss Aussie. I pulled into the alley behind Sin-Sin's house. "Go get your bike." When she fussed again about going, I told her I would tell her father how she'd been gossiping. She frowned up, and then she grinned. Everybody knew how much Sin-Sin liked to announce the news.

We ran into Jeff and Junebug on the way. The four of us tore up the road toward the cemetery. Junebug and Jeff had on their safari hats and combat fatigues. Bunny caught up with us at the stand of palmetto trees rest stop. When I told them that we knew where Dickson's grave was, they said it was about time.

But they seemed excited. We rode up to the cemetery. Miss Effie called to us from her garden where she was weeding her cabbages. She had her straw hat on and was leaning on her hoe. "What're you all fixing to do?"

"We're going to find Gumbo Dickson's grave," we hollered back.

She got down that path faster than I'd ever seen her do. "Let me help. I know exactly where it is." All her wrinkles in her face curled up in a smile. "Hey, Raisin, c'mere and give me a hug."

Glad to see her, but too shamed to hug

her in front of my friends, I just said hi and waved and grinned hard. I hoped she understood.

With Miss Effie in the lead and me, Bunny, Sin-Sin, Junebug, and Jeff following, we trooped into the cemetery. When she stopped suddenly we bumped into one another.

"Praise the Lord!" She pointed with her hoe. "I knew I was right. She was in here doing good. Look here, Raisin, at Gussie Ann's grave!"

Somebody had spruced up her grave. It was encircled by a small white wire fence, new dirt had been tamped down firmly into a neat mound, and a newly planted hydrangea bloomed purple flowers at the head.

"I bet Big Boy did that," I said.

"Big Boy? What the Bear be doing in here?" said Junebug.

"Mind where you are, honey," Miss Effie said. "Yes, 'twas Big Boy. That's her kin there. I saw her come out here three days straight, but I couldn't tell just what she was doing, not to the exact point, you know. I prayed, though, that she was working with this grave."

"Miz Pfluggins," Jeff said. "Mr. Easau said Gumbo Dickson had a house somewhere around where he was buried. Where would it have been? Mr. Easau said it burned down."

"You see where New Africa Number One is falling apart over yonder? That's where his house used to be. His widow deeded all this land from the Big Sing River to over here at the highway to the New Africa congregation." She pulled me to one side. "Read those record books, Raisin!" she whispered. "They'll tell you the whole story! You tell everybody else!"

"I don't want to make people feel bad, though, if it hurts them so bad to remember."

"Oh, honey, I understand. But sometimes people need to remember."

"Miz Pfluggins, do you think Gumbo Dickson's got any relatives left?" Jeff asked.

"I don't believe he does. At least not any left around here. He didn't have any children. No one really knows where he was born." She looked around. "Let me see can I get my bearings. You see over yonder, where some fool piled up that mess of branches and rubbish? I do declare that's where his grave is."

We groaned. The pile of broken flowerpots, entangled vines, papers, beer cans, and other debris must have been three or four feet high and a good ten feet wide. It was the dumping ground.

Swatting at mosquitoes and gnats, we stared at the mess. "We can look around for a granite marker," Miss Effie said, "but I doubt you'll find it anywhere else but under that awful pile of trash."

"We can't let the TV cameras come in and show this," I said.

Miss Effie said that Councilman Ahern called Reverend Walker and wanted to know more about this Mr. Dickson. When Reverend Walker told him where he was buried, Mr. Ahern got off the phone so fast Reverend said he didn't know he'd hung up till he got the dial tone. "Ahern's one of Miss Aussie's side-kicks, you know. She probably got him thinking she came from royalty instead of from right here."

Miss Effie rambled on. We stared at the pile of trash. "Are you sure that's the grave, Miss Effie?" Bunny said under her breath. "Raisin, tell me that's not the spot, please."

"I don't know, but it looks like the middle of the cemetery to me, and that's where the map said he'd be," I whispered back. I was disappointed, too. No matter that I could plainly see the condition the rest of the cemetery was in. I'd had this silly thought that Dickson's grave would stand out in the open just waiting for us to walk up to it.

Finally Jeff went over to the pile and began to pull at some loose branches on top. "Honey, you stay away from there," Miss Effie warned. "Liable to be a rattlesnake ten feet long come running out. You wait till we can get some grown folks out here with strong arms and shotguns and such."

"Plus we gotta wait until the vote comes, hunh," I said.

Miss Effie pursed her lips. "We'll wait till we find out what they're gonna do."

11

That evening Miss Aussie telephoned. What she said to Daddy made him screw up his mouth something awful. "I don't have time to listen to your foolishness," he said and hung up, frowning.

We all went "ohh" under our breath. Ring! I ran to the phone. "Please put your momma on," Miss Aussie snapped. I handed the phone to Momma, who tried to get a word in from the jump—and missed. After about ten minutes of listening, frowning, and screwing up her mouth, too, she broke through.

"You and I been decent friends so far on this cemetery thing, but I'm getting tired of your fussing; it just doesn't make any sense anymore! I think deep down you're scared you won't get any more vote money from those politicians. I know for sure you always told Councilman Ahern you drive Miz Manigo and Miz Kitchen to the polls to vote for him, and they've both been dead and in the grave in that ole cemetery for a good seven years. It'd be too bad for you if he finds out, hunh! Hello, hello?"

She'd hung up on Momma!

Immediately it rang again. Daddy grabbed it up. "Aussie, now you look here! Oh, good evening, Reverend Walker, good evening. I was just hollering after the kids. How're you?"

On Thursday morning I got up early to get a head start on what I wanted to get done, like get ready for Hattie's rehearsal. First I washed my hair good, then rubbed moisturizer into it until the waves came. I wondered if Jeff would think I was cute if I pulled this front handful of hair down over my left eye and put a red streak in just above my right ear. I jerked awake. Girl, quit! I had things to do!

Hattie looked down in the mouth at the kitchen table. When I asked why, Maizell said it was because she had stage fright, which caused her to look even more down in the mouth.

"You'll be all right," I told her. "Everybody

gets nervous their very first time. Tonight the only thing they'll do is find out who everybody is and get them in the right divisions and probably practice the opening number, make you walk right"—I struck my modeling pose, with my hands straight down at my sides, my chin up, and my left foot at a right angle to my other one—"and turn the way you should."

"Is that *all*?" She splatted her spoon into her plate of grits. "I ain't gonna go to no rehearsal and make a fool of myself!"

"After all our work?" Maizell said.

"You don't even have to take your clothes with you or change. Or even do your talent, not tonight. I'm gonna get your shoelaces for your tennis shoes, anyway, just in case you change your mind."

She'd better go! I rolled my eyes at Maizell behind Hattie's back. No confidence!

Before I could get my foot off the front porch step good, Daddy reminded me that I had to weed the okra and tomato patches.

"But my hair'll get all dirty, Daddy! I just washed it!"

He laughed. "Dirty up your hair? I never did see a woman out in the weeds working who didn't have something on her head, especially if she thinks she's got things to do later. So tie up your head, girl, and hit them weeds!"

Phooey!

Two minutes later I was out in the garden wearing my plastic cap, the one that didn't have any holes. I slammed the hoe into the dirt and almost chopped a tomato plant in half. I also needed to wash out some jeans and stop by Bunny's and buy some paper! Doggone these weeds! Just as I reached my third row and had worked up a sweat—thanks to Daddy!— I heard Maizell and Hattie holler at me to come to the house. And hurry!

When I got there, I found everybody crowded around the TV set, where a man stood in a clump of weeds with a microphone in his hand.

"Some say the founder of Gumbo Grove lies in this abandoned cemetery located on the outskirts of the city limits," he said.

The camera focused on the weeds—our weeds! Our cemetery! "In fact, some sources believe that the founder, Alexander Morgan G. Dickson, lies under this pile of unsightly debris"—he pointed to the trash heap, *our* trash heap—"in this cemetery that belongs to New Africa Number One Missionary Baptist Church."

When Miz Skipper's face came on the

screen, Daddy let out a yell. "What's she doing up there? She surely can't be speaking for New Africa!"

"Certainly Mr. Dickson is very, very prominent in this city's history," she was saying in her sticky voice. "But we don't have proof that he is actually in this cemetery. More likely he is located in one further along the Big Sing River."

"Hunh?" we all said.

"Having heard that Gumbo Grove has a famous founder, some residents, like Mrs. Skipper, are now wondering just where he is buried," the reporter said. "At this moment, no one seems to know for sure. For Eye Witness News Sixty-six, this is Jim Booker."

"Oh, you're gonna be busy at that meeting tonight!" I said. "Our cemetery on TV!"

The telephone started up again: about the TV story, about the cemetery, about Miz Skipper. First Momma would answer and fuss, and then Daddy would answer and fuss. We girls sat on the couch and watched and listened. Better than TV!

Daddy finally caught us gawking at them and ordered us back to work.

It wasn't until afternoon that I got to the mall to buy shoelaces for Hattie, who was still wolfing about how she wasn't going to go to rehearsal. I ran into Sin-Sin, DeVera, Chaundra, and the Strickland twins coming out of Palmetto Pastries and Ice Cream. "Girl, I got some hot stuff to tell you," we told each other. We ran back into the ice cream shop, bought ice cream cones, and gossiped down.

When I got back, it was time to get ready for rehearsal. Boy, did Hattie and Momma have a good fight going. As I walked in the door, they finished up a round. Hattie still had "no" written all over her face, and Momma had "yes, you will" on hers. They both turned to me for help.

"Raisin, talk to this child before I get good and mad." Momma had broken out in a sweat. "She's driving me crazy, and I still got to get ready for church."

I sat down on the couch by Hattie, who had her pageant bags stacked up around her. "You don't need to take any of this stuff with you tonight, Hat."

She just kept her lips stuck out, snuffling.

"Bet you're just as nervous as everything, hunh."

"No! Well, yeah, I guess so," she mumbled.

"I was nervous, too, my first time. Everybody is. But you'll probably know everybody there."

"Yeah, but everybody's saying I don't have a talent, and they're gonna laugh."

"You're the one who wanted to sing 'Telephone Man' and wear purple socks. I thought you wanted people to laugh at you. You wanted to tell jokes, didn't you?"

"I don't wanna go anymore."

I sighed. "Hat, look. You wanted to be in it, so come on tonight and be in it. After tonight, if you don't want to, maybe Momma'll let you quit, okay? First-night jitters is no big thing. Okay?"

She blew out her breath, thinking, and finally said okay.

Whee, look at me go! I was proud I got that solved so quickly. Momma breathed out a sigh of relief and smiled at me as I went past for the bathroom to do a quick wash-up.

Rehearsal was at the high school just up the road from church. Momma and Daddy let us out first. "And, Raisin, make her stand up straight," Momma said as they drove off.

"Don't nobody better say a word about my purple stockings," Hattie warned us. "I like purple and that's that."

We stood at the back of the auditorium and looked around first so that Hattie wouldn't feel so nervous. Girls stood on stage, hung off the banisters, or slouched in the aisles and in the seats. Mothers pulled on their little girls to make them sit down. And noisy! But I still wished I could have gone to the church meeting and watched the fireworks.

Miss Wilhemena Birdsong, the pageant director, flitted from one side of the auditorium to the other with a yellow legal pad in her hand. "Deidra, leave the lights alone, honey! Where's Timika Bellamy? Libby. Chaundra. I need your money before Friday, all right?"

Deidra, the star of the show in *her* mind, stood on stage and fussed at Jeff, who was in the balcony working the spotlight. "I want pink when I sing my song, and I want blue when I come out in my formal," she announced.

Hattie wouldn't walk to the front of the auditorium. "I can't sing in a pink light," she grumbled.

"You can change it," I told her. "Just tell Jeff. He'll get that all worked out in plenty of time."

Libby Burns swept through the doors. "Oh, Hattie, they said you dropped out," she lisped through her retainer. "When'd you get back in?"

"I didn't drop out!"

"Well, you're back in, so good," she said. "I guess maybe you finally got enough ads to qualify. See ya!"

"Who said I dropped out?"

I pushed Hattie ahead of me. "Don't pay her any attention. You know how she just likes to intimidate people."

But it was like that all the way to the front: some girl would say something to Hattie, and Hattie would get upset. "Chill out," Maizell said to her. "They ain't being mean."

Mary Elouise, one of Hattie's actual friends, came over and sat down by her. "Did you get an ad from Latimer's Funeral Home?"

"And one from McKiever's and Nelson's and a half page from Miz Irene's BarBQue Pit," Hattie said. She started to look like she was ready to relax.

Mary Elouise was suitably impressed. Then she eyed Hattie's bags. "Why'd you bring all that stuff? Your dress in there? Lemme see." She pulled at a bag. "It's that pink one, right? The one you were bawling over so 'cause you thought your momma wouldn't—"

"Here." Hattie shoved the right bag at her before Mary Elouise could finish.

"Girls, girls, come on, come on!" Miss Wilhemena flew through us. Then, waving her arms, she hopped up on stage.

She rolled off a humongous list of what she wanted us—I mean them—to do and how she wanted it done. Of course, we didn't pay her any attention. Not on the first go-round—tradition, you know. Before the real pageant came off, Miss Whilhemena would have changed things three or four times. So we kept talking, walking around, singing, and Maizell and I reassuring Hattie.

"I said, let's get *started*!" she shouted.

Now it was time to get started.

"Hat, listen good now so you'll know what to do," Maizell said.

Just then Jeff wandered over. He looked like a tourist in his white golfing shirt, white shorts, and golfer's white visor. Looked just as fine as could be, even though he did have skinny legs. I was pleased that he came to talk to me. "What do you think they're doing over at church?" he asked me.

"I don't know, but if I had the nerve I'd sneak over there and see."

I saw DeVera look our way two or three times and wave to him. So I thought of something fast to keep him with me. "Did you see the story on TV about the cemetery? How'd they find out about it?"

"Well, I asked Miz Pennyfeather about him after I read her column. I bet she told Channel Sixty-six. You know how she likes to promote everything! Daddy said Miz Skipper got on TV because she just *happened* to drive past when she saw the cameraman." He grinned. "If Miz Pennyfeather hadn't done it, then I think I would, just to help you out, you know."

I was impressed. Help me out! I couldn't help but smile back as pretty at him as I could. I was glad my curls were still in place.

"Girls, girls! You're not listening!" Miss Wilhemena shouted from on stage. "Shush up! I need to announce something first, and then we'll get started with the Little Misses and their walk. As you know, Miz Alfronia DeCosta Meriwether founded this pageant twenty-seven years ago. This year the pageant committee has decided to give a community service award called the Miz Alfronia DeCosta Meriwether Community Service Award. Isn't that wonderful?"

When we all kept quiet and didn't say anything, Miss Wilhemena added, "It'll be one hundred dollars in cash."

We all yelled at that!

"Little Miss Ebony contestants, I want you to line up on stage here right now," she said.

"That's you, Hattie," Maizell said. "Go on!"

"I don't wanna do it." Hattie scrouched down in the seat and clung to the arms.

"If you don't get up on that stage I'm gonna tell everybody that you're a scaredy-cat," said Maizell.

"No!"

Six girls trooped up to the stage while Maizell, Hattie, and I argued. Miss Wilhemena looked down at us. "Hattie, please come up here, too, honey."

Hattie shook her head.

"Hattie," said Miss Wilhemena, "I hear you've got such a nice walk. I want you to help me show the others, okay?"

Hattie's mouth fell open. "Me?"

"Go on, girl!" we said, trying to keep the surprise off our faces. Hattie got up slowly from her seat and tiptoed toward the stage.

"But you've got to walk faster than that," Miss Wilhemena said. "C'mon, helper, help me!"

Hattie broke into a big grin and hurried up on stage.

"I like your stockings," Miss Wilhemena said.

First the girls had to learn to walk straight, arms parallel to their legs, shoulders back, chin up. They had to know what stage left, stage center, and stage right meant.

"Now everybody look this way and smile!" Miss Wilhemena commanded. Mary Elouise and Hattie got confused and ended up with their backs to the audience. "Where's my helper? Hattie? Let's try it again," Miss Wilhemena chirped. "Step and turn, two, three, four. Try to walk in a line. Don't take long steps! Keep a smile on your face! Stop and turn. You'll get it!"

After rehearsal ended, I looked around for Momma and saw her sitting in the back row. I ran up the aisle, but Hattie beat me to her. "Momma, I was so good! Miss Wilhemena made me her helper. I had to show everybody else how to walk."

Momma looked at me for confirmation, and I nodded. "Well, good for you. So you like it and you're gonna stay in?"

"I guess so," Hattie said. "Maybe."

"Well, Raisin, nothing much happened on my end except that they fussed and fussed," Momma said later. "We have to meet again tomorrow night to decide on the cemetery." She hesitated. "But they did elect a secretary. And Raisin, it's for the best."

"Miss Effie didn't win, hunh." Miss Aussie? Oh, no!

"Well, they nominated Miss Effie, but she withdrew her name and had us put Miz Thomas's name in her place. Miss Effie said she was too old and too tired to keep on being secretary. So we elected Miz Thomas. Miz Skipper didn't get over ten votes."

Jeff's momma secretary? All right! What

a turnabout, for true. But what about the cemetery?

Early the next morning the telephone woke me up. I heard Momma say, "I see, I see, I see. Oh, don't feel that way. Raisin's up. I'll get her. Raisin!"

I straggled out of bed, wondering who wanted me so early. Miss Effie. Before I got a chance to congratulate her, she got started about the cemetery. "That television story didn't help much," she said. "It just don't look good. Miz Skipper talked half the night at church about how Gumbo Dickson wasn't in our cemetery and couldn't anybody prove it unless they showed her the grave. She's still trying to get it torn up and moved."

"Well, can't we find the grave? The record books show where he's buried."

"But, baby, I still can't get anybody to come out and help clean up the cemetery!" Her voice went high. "All those folks at church last night and not a one volunteered to help. Everybody's just talking and no doing."

I hung up and turned to Momma in panic. "We gotta help Miss Effie clean up the cemetery today, before you vote on what to do with it tonight."

"I'd love to help, but not today. I don't have much time today to do anything but clean

condos. And I need you to help me. You best
stay out of that ole snakey cemetery. She should
have made an announcement last night at
church about needing help."

"But she said nobody volunteered!"

"Yeah, but you gotta speak up when you
want things done. She sat right there and didn't
put out a peep about asking anybody. Now,
quick, you go get me some salt from Mr.
Easau's. Here's a dollar. And you come right
back, hear?"

I stamped out of the house and hopped
on my bike, burning mad. Why couldn't Momma
help? She said she would! But not today! Just
like Miss Effie said! All talk and no do!

I rode up the street as fast as I could, then
shot onto Fifteenth Street. Jeff and Walter Bill
stood by Mr. Easau at the Gumbo Limbo.

"What're you so frowned up about?" Mr.
Easau asked when I got there.

"Nobody's gonna help in the cemetery and
nobody cares," I told him, "and I want some
salt."

"You look salty enough now," he said and
gave out a big shout of laughter.

"She looks like she's gonna cry," Walter
Bill added.

"I do not!" I blinked back the hot tears.
"All this talk goes on about how everybody

wants to do, but when the time comes nobody's around to do it!"

"Oh, my," Mr. Easau said, still laughing. "Well, you say what you need done right this minute and I'll help you do it."

I looked him square in the eye. "I want to find Gumbo Dickson's grave and clean up the cemetery."

"Oh, well." He scratched his chin.

"See! You, too!"

"Whoa, now, there's no need to yell. I'm on your side." He shrugged. "So let's get started!"

"What? You can help? For real?" But then I fell back. "But *I* can't even help because Momma says the cemetery is too snakey. We need some grown folks in there, she said."

"I got a .410 shotgun that'll take care of any snakes. And I'll call your momma and dad and talk to 'em, and Reverend Walker, too, and see can't I round up some folks. We can be the slowest people on God's creation when it comes to getting things done for ourselves sometimes. Go there, y'all, and get those hoes and shovels and rakes out the back of the shop and put 'em in my truck."

"I'll call Momma and see can she or Dad help, too," Jeff said.

"And call Bunny, too!" I took off for the

rakes. "And I heard that your mom got elected—arrgh!"

I saw stars.

When my eyes focused, I was looking up at Big Boy looking down at me. I was on the ground. "You oughta honk when you come around corners," I said, sitting up. When I felt the back of my head for bumps, I pulled a handful of dirt and grass out of my hair.

She helped me up. "Where you goin' so fast that you ain't lookin'?"

"Going to clean up the cemetery. Wanna help?"

"Shuh, I ain't getting my hands dirty."

"Look at *me* all covered with yuck after you run over me. Plus, didn't you clean up Gussie Ann's grave?"

"Who told you that?"

"I just know. It looks really nice. You oughta come. Or do you think your grandmother will get after you?"

"She can't get after me for nothin' if I wanna do it." Big Boy stamped off.

I got the hoes and carried them back to the truck where Walter Bill hauled them up. I wished Big Boy would come, too. We needed all the help we could get.

In a few minutes Crackers thundered into the yard on his Harley Davidson. He pulled off his sunglasses and his black gloves. "Hey, little momma, what it is," he said to me from under his brown beret. He went into the store and in a few minutes came back out. "Tell me something good."

"Hey, we're working, that's what!" Jeff hollered loudly from the telephone booth. He eyed Crackers like Crackers was a thief. "C'mon, Raisin, you ready?"

I looked at Jeff in surprise. Since when . . . ? I smiled at Crackers just as nicely as I could, proud that people said I had pretty white straight teeth. "We could use your big, strong muscles to help us clean the cemetery."

He dimpled back to me. "Oh, that's right. You're into that Gumbo Dickson bag, hunh. Sure, little momma, I'll be there." He roared off.

I clapped my hands and gave a little scream inside. Momma was so right, you *can* catch more flies with honey than you can with vinegar.

Jeff came over and said Bunny and Sin-Sin would try to come. "What're you doing talking to Crackers like that? He's an old man." He cocked his safari hat low over his eyes and then looked down at me. I could see his jaw muscles tightening and untightening.

"Oh, Jeff, I just asked him a question!

C'mon, we've got work to do!" I had to smile pretty at him, too. Jealous? Did that mean he liked me?

Mr. Easau came out of his shop with his shotgun, then padlocked shut the door. "I talked with your daddy, Raisin, and he said he understood just how this thing was so important to you. So you can come on. Yes, I thought that would make you grin. And he said he and your momma'll come help, too. He said them condos would have to wait."

Quickly we loaded up the truck with tools. Bunny and Sin-Sin, too, puffed up the road and then hauled themselves into the truck with us. "Pooch and Candy wanted to come, too," Bunny said, "but Momma was 'wake and in a good mood. She said she'd look after them."

Sin-Sin kicked my shoe with her foot. "You realize I got to be *awful* bored to come out to a cemetery again."

"You and me both," Bunny said. "This girl is crazy, I swear. Chasing after ghosts, digging in cemeteries. Remember last time when she wanted us to help save the whales and sea turtles? And when she made us go out and make fools of ourselves trying to run for muscular dystrophy?"

"Crackers said he was coming," I told them.

"Girl, I wouldn't miss this for the world!" Bunny screamed. "Start up this truck!"

Mr. Easau set a case of Coke beside us. "In case y'all get thirsty."

We rattled past Fifteenth Street to Lebo's corner where, in the middle of a roll of dust, Mr. Lebo was sweeping his yard. I saw him brush the broom over two guys leaning against the wall of his café to make them move. Mr. Easau slowed his truck. "Sure could use that broom over at the old cemetery. C'mon, broom! Lebo, you can come, too!"

"That your crew?" Mr. Lebo squinted at us. "Pygmies. Take two of them to handle this broom."

"That's why I hope that broom will bring you, too!"

Mr. Lebo and Mr. Easau laughed. Mr. Lebo and the two guys got into Mr. Lebo's truck and came along after us.

I was so excited I couldn't see straight. Help was on the way!

"Daddy said he was coming," Sin-Sin said.

"But you know, if enough folks show up, we can get that place cleaned up in one day," Mr. Easau hollered back at us.

"But if people vote it down tonight, then I'll be done just sweated and broke my fingernails working in that graveyard for nothing," Sin-Sin said.

"Oh, girl, you can be so negative," Bunny said, watching me. "Gimme a break, hunh?"

Reverend Walker, my folks and our truck, and some others were already at the cemetery when we drove up. Miss Effie had come out, too. "Praise the Lord," she said when she saw me. She pulled me off the truck hugging me. "Just look what you done!"

Miss Effie, Momma, Miz Thomas, and Reverend Walker quickly organized us. Grown-ups were to cut and chop, and shoo snakes. Us kids were to tote trash to the trucks.

When Crackers rode up, Bunny raced over to me and dug her fingernails in my arm. "Girl, I got to have some of that!" she squealed.

"Bunny, you ought to quit." I laughed, struggling to free my arm. I saw Jeff watching me. I waved at him. "C'mon, let's get to work."

Of course, the first thing we all decided to do was see what was under that big trash pile.

Miss Effie, who had been giving directions with her hoe and her hat, leaned over to me. "Take a look at what drove up by the fence," she said. It was WWGG-TV 66, and Jim Booker was unloading camera equipment.

"How could he know?"

She beamed. "Press always knows, honey. It's just getting them to do that's hard."

Bunny and I went back to work dragging limbs across the ground, but we kept an eye on Booker, hoping he would aim his camera at us. He didn't. A blue Toyota pulled up behind the TV car. Miz Pennyfeather! She picked her way through the weeds, smiling and nodding at everyone. When she saw me, she lifted up one end of a big branch and helped me carry it to the truck.

More and more people came, some to help, some to look. Deacon Rapture showed up, looking sour, but he even picked up a few broken flowerpots and threw them on the truck.

"Miss Effie, who's that?" I pointed to a tall, bald-headed White man carefully stepping through the weeds.

"That's Wim Smithers, president of the Calvary County Historical Society, and a good friend. He's known about Gumbo Dickson for years, but he stayed a tight-mouthed man about it. He said Our Own ought to be the ones to speak up for Our Own."

"Look, they're getting close to the bottom!" We crowded in by Jeff and Bunny to see.

Reverend Walker lifted off the remains of a Christmas tree with paper icicles still dangling off the branches and pushed aside a matted mess of stalks. He raked hard.

"Here!" Miss Effie elbowed her way into the clearing and with Mr. Lebo's broom swept the ground. "Here! Here! Here he is! Praise the Lord!"

I pushed in, too. There it was—a blackened stone marker lying flat in the brown sand. But was that really him? I got to my knees and with a sharp stick dug at the dirt clogging the stone letters. My heart beat so fast I could barely breathe. A few letters came up: A-L-E. I dug quicker: X-A-N-D-E-R! M-O-R-G-A-N! G. D-I-C-K-S-O-N!

I must have leaped ten feet in the air.

I grabbed Miss Effie's hands and swung her around. Her hat went back on her head. Daddy pounded Reverend Walker on the back. Mr. Easau took hold of Jeff and Bunny and held their arms up high. Momma rushed in and hugged me and Miss Effie both, while Miz Pennyfeather reached in and patted me on the shoulder.

"Well, isn't this a grand day!" Reverend Walker said over and over. "We should all be very proud of this discovery."

Bunny and Jeff and Sin-Sin and I yelled and yelled just to do it, and jumped around.

Please, Lord, I said inside, please make this save the cemetery!

After we had all quieted down, Reverend Walker led us in a short prayer. "And I might add that I, for one, will do my utmost to keep our cemetery right here and give the city's fine founder the kind of memorial he is due."

"I'll certainly second that," Mr. Smithers said.

"Hey, wait a minute." Jim Booker jumped down from where he had been standing on a stump, filming everything. "If the founder is in this cemetery, then you must mean that the founder of Gumbo Grove was Black."

He rushed over and stuck his microphone first in front of Mr. Smithers and then in front of Reverend Walker. Mr. Smithers just shook his head until Miss Effie poked him with her finger.

"A-hum. Well, it's common knowledge about Mr. Dickson," Mr. Smithers began. He hesitated. Miss Effie poked him again.

"We've spoke up for Our Own. Now you speak up," she whispered.

"Yes, well, unh, Mr. Dickson was Black. Yes. But the time had never, unh, been appropriate to give him the credit that Mr. Dickson merits." He looked at Miss Effie, who smiled and nodded. "But that time is past due, and I intend to do all that I can, as president of the Calvary County Historical Society, to help all of you in your endeavors. That is, if you plan to keep the cemetery here and can vouch for its maintenance and its, unh, inhabitants."

"Oh, I'm sure we will," Reverend Walker said. The camera swung to him. "I'm sure we will. It would be a disgrace and a slap in the face to the city, to the state, to the nation, and to our ancestors if we disturbed their graves. And I'm confident the vote tonight will support the cemetery. I plan to talk with the mayor. All of our councilmen, including Mr. Fence, our city councilman who is a member of New Africa, and Mr. Ahern over there, will want to push to get the full support of the city in this project as well."

I looked around in amazement when Reverend Walker mentioned Councilman Fence. He was here, too? And Mr. Ahern? They were Miz Skippers' sidekicks and did whatever she said. And then I noticed that behind me there must have been a good fifty or more people. And more reporters. I knew because they had notepads and tape recorders. There was even a TV reporter here from Myrtle Beach!

That's when I began to feel warm inside.

People were finally here to help. Just two weeks ago there had been only Miss Effie and me and Maizell. And Big Boy. I slipped my arm through Miss Effie's. "We got some help now, don't we?"

"Yes, baby," she said, and all her wrinkles crinkled up. "You're such a wonderful child. You made all this happen. You and that history!"

She told me that the next thing we needed to do was to go to the printers and have them make copies of every page in the record books. "You keep a copy, I'll keep a copy, and then we'll turn the books over to Miz Thomas."

Suddenly she nudged me. "Well, will you look yonder?"

Big Boy! Miz Skipper! Who didn't look as sticky and sly as usual. In fact, she looked like she was about to come apart in the face. Her mouth was partly open, and her eyes were bugging out.

Mr. Ahern and Mr. Fence saw her, too. "Come on, come on," Reverend Walker hollered at her when Mr. Fence pointed. Miz Skipper shook her head. She looked like she was trying to get back into her car, but Big Boy had her by the arm and was trying to drag her into the cemetery. Mr. Ahern hurried over to Miz Skipper. Taking her firmly by the elbow that Big Boy had held, he brought her over to us. She didn't look happy about *that* at all.

"Miz Skipper, I just wanted you to know that I found something of *great* interest in this cemetery," he told her. "Let me show you."

"No, I—"

"Here, come right here!" Still holding her arm, Mr. Ahern dragged her right over to Gussie Ann's grave. "They tell me this grave is one of the oldest in here. This is so historical, don't you think?"

"Well, I—"

"Historical," Mr. Fence said. "I think it is, too."

"You know, the city can make a major contribution to the development of this cemetery. Do you know how?"

Miz Skipper looked at him so sad and fearful like she didn't want to hear anymore. "How, Councilman?" She let out a loud sigh.

"Because the city can get state funds."

Her face went blank, then sly. "Oh, you can?"

"Oh, sure. Such antiquity, don't you agree? See, every family that has relatives here will probably get some kind of financial assistance to fix up the graves."

"They will? Then I'll handle that part."

Mr. Fence shook his head. "No, I will. I'm on the City Council. You're not."

Suddenly Miz Skipper saw me looking at her. "Oh, Raisin, come here and let me shake your hand for doing such a good job with this cemetery."

I didn't want to go over, but Momma gave me a little push from behind. After all the mess Miz Skipper had caused, it seemed like she wouldn't have come anywhere close to the cemetery.

"Young lady, you've done a splendid job," Mr. Ahern said. "Tell me, have you considered running for City Council? We need leaders like you."

I just shook my head, embarrassed and pleased.

"Tell me, Raisin, what is the history behind this grave? Someone's been in here and really made it look nice." Mr. Ahern pointed at Gussie Ann Vereen's grave.

I sucked in my breath and looked over at Miz Skipper. She just looked back at me with that sticky smile pasted on her lips. It seemed a little twisted right now, though. I turned around and looked at Momma, who had heard every word. She smiled a little, but that's all. "I don't know, Mr. Ahern," I finally said. "You'll have to ask Miss Effie. Or Miz Skipper."

Mr. Ahern laughed. "Oh, come on, Raisin. You're the little historian. Tell us."

By now lots of people had come around to listen. I looked back at Miz Skipper. Her mouth worked, but nothing came out. She looked all broken up in her face, like her tooth hurt, and she was in bad pain. What should I do? If I told the truth . . . I remembered the look on Daddy's face when he told me about crying when he was a little boy, and about people wanting to forget the pain. And then I remembered what Miss Effie said about sometimes people need to remember the pain, so they won't forget. But I didn't want to hurt Miz Skipper, not really.

"Miss Effie?" I turned to her for help.

Miss Effie beamed at me. "Mr. Ahern, Raisin doesn't know the history as well as I and Miz Skipper know it. You tell him, Miz Skipper."

Miz Skipper put her hand to her throat and played with her necklace. "Well, I expect that some would say she had kin in Gumbo Grove," she said. "But I'll have to check the record books and see for sure. These graves are very, very old, you know, and records and such can get lost."

"I'll be glad to check that for you," said

Miz Thomas, our new church secretary. "I'm sure everything is in those books."

Miz Skipper looked mean for a minute, and then it just seemed like her face fell apart. She tried to put a little saggy smile on her face for Mr. Ahern. "Well, if you look, you might find some reference to me in her history. They say she's kin to me."

Mr. Ahern said, "I see!"

He took hold of her elbow and smiled. "And I meant to ask you about those graves I found over here," he said, "by the names of Manigo and Kitchen."

"Oh," Miz Skipper said, "you'll need to talk to Mr. Fence about that."

"I don't think I'm familiar with those names," Mr. Fence said quickly.

Miss Effie winked at me, and we giggled together.

We did it, we did it! I kept saying to myself. Jeff came over to me and put his safari hat on my head.

"Just in case you get too hot," he said, grinning.

I told Miss Effie that Jeff had an old book that told about Gumbo Dickson. She seemed very pleased and surprised, and asked him to let her see it sometime.

We went back to work, and this time Big
Boy joined us. She could carry three times as
much as the rest of the kids. She and Crackers,
who was really grown.

I grinned at Big Boy, glad to see her there
to help, and told her so.

"Well, don't anybody better say anything
bad about Gussie neither," she said, "else they're
gonna have to get up with me."

"Yes, Lord, help them if they do," Bunny
whispered behind me. We dragged limbs across
the ground to the truck. Big Boy grabbed an
end and helped me carry it on. And when I
looked around me, I saw Miz Skipper. She had
picked up a branch and was toting it, too.

Pageant Time!

The house was in a hurricane all day: "Get Hattie to Miss Erma's by nine o'clock, Raisin, so she can do something with that hair."

"And, Raisin, be sure she keeps that medicine on those legs, too."

"And, Maizell, please remind her to stand straight!"

"And, Raisin, please go to the cleaners and get my dress!"

"Maizell, you'll have to take care of the garbage 'cause Hattie and I have a long date with some bubble bath!"

Maizell and Hattie had practiced the telephone song over and over and over, with

Maizell reminding Hattie how to do the dance steps they'd learned from watching "Soul Train" and the other music shows. I was surprised. Maizell had been able to teach Hattie a lot about dancing. Hattie looked halfway decent. Not great, but decent, you know?

Four-thirty. In another hour and a half we had to be at the school. Hurry! So much to do! Momma was like a chicken with her head cut off, just like she had been with me. Hattie was right with her, too. And which dress did I want to wear? Which heels?

We were all so pleased with Hattie deciding to stay in the pageant. She was even willing to represent Nigeria in the parade-of-countries opening number. See, every girl chose a country to represent from names drawn out of a hat. Sometimes when girls drew an African country, they'd try to switch with somebody else. They wouldn't know how to dress African, and they thought somebody might make fun of them if they dressed in costume. But Hattie said it was fine with her 'cause she had seen pictures of Africans wearing sundresses and shorts, just like everybody else.

"Are we all ready?"

I slipped on my shoes and, smoothing down my skirt, hurried into the living room. Momma had on her favorite blue flowered sundress and Daddy wore his blue dress shirt and a bow tie. Maizell was ready in a beige and brown culotte outfit.

Hattie had on a white sundress and white sandals. Miss Erma had given Hattie curls all over her head. Her legs looked smooth and shiny.

"Hattie, you look so pretty!" I said.

She grinned. "I'm about scared to death."

"You're gonna do fine," Momma said. "Just remember everything you're suppose to do."

"Well, I ain't gonna win anything, anyway."

"Don't think like that," Maizell said. "You might, if you try."

"Yeah, I'm gonna try, but I know I won't win," she said.

We piled in the truck and drove to the school. Lots of cars were already there. Momma and Maizell took Hattie to the back of the stage. Daddy and I found some seats at the front, and waited. Daddy fiddled with his camera. "I hope I can remember how to work this thing," he said.

Quickly the auditorium filled with parents, friends, other kids, people from everywhere! I saw Jeff in the balcony working the spotlight. He had on his beige suit.

I saw Miss Effie come in, too. She had her fur draped around her neck, to show she was *really* dressed up. She sat down in the front row, where the other members of the Calvary County Negro Business and Professional Women's Club—wearing their furs, too—were seated.

"Won't they get hot?" I asked.

"You'd think so," Daddy said.

The lights dimmed. Music came over the loudspeakers. That meant it was almost time to start. Our pageant almost always started on time, but a lot of others would be half an hour or even an hour late.

Though I wanted to be backstage, I wanted to be here, too. I looked at the program that Junebug, who was an usher, had given me.

Mistress of ceremonies was Miss Twyla Jeanette Reynolds, who was Miss Palmetto, from Elgin, S.C. When she came out on stage, everybody applauded. She was tall, dark brown–skinned, and had dimples. She flashed everybody a big smile and waved. I thought she was the most beautiful queen I'd ever seen.

"Good evening, ladies and gentlemen, and welcome to the Twenty-seventh Annual Miss Ebony Calvary County Pageant," she began

"Good luck, Hattie," I whispered.

The music struck up a quick beat. "Ladies

and gentlemen, here they come," said Miss Palmetto, "our contestants for this year's pageant, visiting you from all around the world!"

The girls trooped in pairs from the back of the auditorium, with Mary Elouise and Hattie leading the way and singing to the music. Each girl carried a basket that told which country she represented. Hattie looked so pretty in her sundress and hat. Her basket had "Nigeria" printed on it in big blue letters. She stood straight, too!

They marched up the stage, then divided into three lines, one on each side of the stage and one in the middle. Mary Elouise kept wrinkling up her nose. Hattie stood as still as a stone.

"Smile, Hattie," I said under my breath. I pointed to my mouth, but I guess she couldn't see me.

The curtains opened to reveal a collage of flags from around the world suspended from the ceiling. They hung in front of a large cardboard backdrop of blue mountains, green lakes and yellow sand. It was a gorgeous set. We all applauded.

"The theme for our pageant, as you know, is always 'To Be Young, Gifted and Black,' " said Miss Palmetto. "These wonderful young ladies whom you see here tonight all represent that theme. They are definitely positive images. Let's give them a hand!

"Our first contestant in the Little Miss Ebony category is Mary Elouise Avery."

When Miss Palmetto spoke her name, Mary Elouise stepped forward to the middle of the stage, paused, turned, then walked to the right, paused, and then to the left. She forgot to pause there, though. As she walked, Miss Palmetto explained who Mary Elouise was, what she liked to do, and which country she represented. Mary Elouise represented the Bahamas, "where we are young, gifted and Black," Miss Palmetto finished. "Please give her some applause."

When Hattie's name was called, she came to the front of the stage, but instead of pausing, she hurried on to the right, and then to the left. Just then, she remembered. Turning back around, Hattie walked to the front of the stage, looked down, and threw out one of the prettiest smiles I've ever seen her give. Daddy scrambled to his feet and snapped off a picture.

Everybody broke into applause just as Miss Palmetto said, "And she represents Nigeria, where we are young, gifted and Black." She didn't need to ask us to applaud. Hattie looked great!

When all of the girls had been introduced,

Miss Palmetto told us about the contest itself and the prizes. In Hattie's category, for six- to ten-year-olds, first prize was a $25 gift certificate, a radio, a trophy, and some flowers. For Junior Miss, eleven to fifteen, first prize was $100, a trophy, and flowers. For Miss, from sixteen to twenty-one years, first prize was a $500 scholarship to the college of your choice, a trophy, and flowers. And all the winners got to preside at special programs. When there were parades, the Miss Ebony queens got to ride on their own floats. If Hattie won, she'd get to be in the parades, too. As for me, well, wait till next year!

All the girls walked off the stage, and the curtains closed. I looked around to see if Sin-Sin and Bunny were there. There was Bunny! I waved at her, trying not to be impolite to the people around me.

Next on the program was sportswear. After that would be talent, formal wear, and questions, which were hard. You picked a question from a box, gave it to the M.C., who read it to you out loud. You only had about five seconds to think of an answer. Some girls couldn't think of anything to say. I wondered how Hattie would do.

Talent time! I crossed my fingers. Deidra came out in her pink outfit, smiling like she was ready to stun the world. I had to hand it to her: she could sing, and she didn't need to lip-sync. Hattie had a lot of stiff competition, from her and from Libby, from Timika—well, from all of them.

I saw Momma come down the steps by the stage. She hurried over to us and sat down.

"Hattie looks good, Momma," I said.

"You got to come backstage right now," she whispered. "Hattie has froze up again and wants to drop out!" She jumped back up, heading for the stairs, and I followed.

Oh, Hattie, I groaned inside. What now?

Backstage, girls and mothers and sisters and aunts and friends rushed back and forth, dresses and stockings and shorts in their hands and arms.

"Where's my toe shoes for my dance?" said Timika, who took ballet.

"Can I borrow your hairbrush just a second?" Chaundra's mother asked somebody.

Hattie sat in a corner by a pile of rope, dressed in her purple stockings, pink knickers, high-top tennis shoes, purple shirt, and black beret. Her lips stuck out. She was frowned up hard.

"What's the matter?" I asked. "You can't quit now!"

Hattie just rolled her eyes and stayed put.

"They're going to announce her any minute," Momma said, wringing her hands. "Hattie, come on!"

"Where's your music?" I asked her, but she wouldn't even look at me.

"Crackers has it," Maizell said. "Hattie, you don't wanna be a quitter. Come on!"

Libby went past us. "Hattie, are you ready to sing? Or did you change your mind? You little kids get scared to be on stage. I'm not."

Hattie jumped up. "You ain't no older than I am, Libby. You think you're so cute!"

"Hattie!" Momma hissed.

Miss Wilhemena, who had been watching, hurried up to us. "Hattie, honey, I was just *so* pleased with your walking. Now keep it up with your talent. Come on, come on!"

She grabbed Hattie by the hand and swept her out to the middle of the stage behind the curtains. Then, before Hattie could dash back off, the curtains opened. "And now, ladies and gentlemen, Hattie Stackhouse singing, 'Telephone Man.' "

I hurried back to my seat. Hattie stood like a statue in the middle of the stage. The music began, but Hattie didn't. The audience began to titter.

Come on, Hattie! I shook my hands, trying to get her attention, then I ran to the steps leading backstage.

Maizell rushed to the wings. "Hattie! Look at me! Look! C'mon!" She began to do Hattie's routine, dancing her legs off behind the curtains and mouthing the words to the song.

Like she was coming out of a trance, slowly Hattie began to dance. Watching Maizell, she swooped and crouched and then acted like she held a telephone in her hand. The audience began to clap in time to the music.

I watched Maizell, too. The girl was good! I realized then that she should have been in the pageant instead of Hattie. And I also told myself that it would be better the next year for Maizell to have her chance. I'd already had mine.

With a flourish, Maizell and Hattie finished the dance. The audience whooped and whistled and clapped. Hattie ran off the stage and into our arms. "You did good, you really did!" Momma said.

"Yeah, thanks to Maizell," Hattie said, hugging us back. "Thanks, Maizell."

The end of the pageant neared. All the girls marched on the stage in their formal wear to strut their stuff.

Bunny slid into the seat by me. "How do you think she's doing?" she asked.

"I'm pretty sure she should get some kind of mention. Keepin' my fingers crossed for queen, too." I tried not to sound too proud. "I think she even might make second runner-up. Deidra has got the crown, and first place'll probably go to Libby or Timika, unless they score low on their questions or talent. I think they brought in the same amount of ad money as Hattie."

"Well, maybe they will. But I think Hattie did a good job. She sure is a lot better than she was when she started out."

"You're right about that."

That very same night, I just remembered, the Miss Cherry Bomb Pageant was being held at the civic center. I hoped it went off with a bang! I had to giggle. Calvary County had more pageants than any other county in the state, but the Cherry Bomb Pageant was the funniest one I'd ever heard of.

Mary Elouise Avery came out wearing a white taffeta dress with matching lace anklets, black patent-leather pumps, and white gloves. She marched around the stage, smiling, her arms stiff at her sides. "This is Mary Elouise Avery," Miss Palmetto said. "She's nine years old and in third grade at Gumbo Grove Elementary. Mary Elouise likes to double dutch, play softball, and watch television. Her favorite color is white, which she is wearing, and her favorite hero is the Reverend Jesse Jackson. Thank you, Mary Elouise."

Libby Burns came out in a shiny lavender dress, black pumps, and a garland of lavender and white flowers in her hair, which was styled in a pageboy. She had lipstick on, too, and powder. "Libby Burns is eight years old and in third grade at Gumbo Grove Elementary. She likes to play tennis, swim, and play records. Her favorite color is yellow, and her favorite hero is Whitney Houston. Thank you, Libby Burns."

Hattie came out in her pink dress and matching anklets. The skirts stood out so stiffly that she looked just like a store doll. Miss Erma had made her hair look really pretty, too. It was really hard to believe that this was our same old head-hard-as-a-rock Hattie. "Hattie Stackhouse is eight years old and in third grade, also at Gumbo Grove Elementary. Hattie says she likes to ride her bike, watch television, go crabbing, and do cheerleading jumps. Her favorite color is purple, and her favorite hero is also the Reverend Jesse Jackson. Thank you, Hattie Stackhouse."

Deidra's sky-blue chiffon dress was like a fairy's, with glitter sprinkled over it. The powder-blue sash complementing it hung down in back and swished when she moved.

"Who is that one?" somebody said.

"I forgot, but I'm glad I'm not competing with her," somebody else said. "I sure Lord would be in trouble."

Miss Palmetto held out the box of questions to Mary Elouise, who drew a slip of paper and handed it to her. "Your question is, What would you do if you caught your best friend cheating on a test?" she asked. "Now, I'll repeat that. What would you do if you caught your best friend cheating on a test?"

"What would I do if I caught my best friend cheating on a test," Mary Elouise repeated. Everything got silent.

"Poor Mary Elouise," Bunny whispered. "I know she didn't want to get *that* question after they had a big stink not long ago when they caught her sister cheating at Florida State."

"Well, I would . . . unh, unh . . . I'd . . ." Mary Elouise tried to answer. We all waited, feeling sorry for her. I could see tears in her eyes, too. "Unh. If . . . unh, I don't know."

"You don't know?" said Miss Palmetto, who didn't know about the stink.

"No, ma'am, I don't know what I would do."

"That sure didn't help her," said Bunny.

Miss Palmetto held out the box of questions to Libby, who reached in, pulled one out, and handed it to her. Miss Palmetto read the question: "If you could have any animal in the world to be your pet, what would you have, and why?"

"I'd have an elephant," said Libby proudly, lifting her nose in the air.

"And why?" Miss Palmetto asked, turning the microphone back to her.

"Because it has a long nose," said Libby.

"Just like yours!" I heard a boy behind me say real loud. Everybody laughed. I giggled, but Libby stamped her foot angrily.

"That didn't help her, either," Bunny said again.

"No, but it might help Hattie," Daddy said, overhearing us. "C'mon, Hattie, you always got an answer for everything."

"Hattie, your question is, If you had a million dollars but couldn't spend it on yourself, what would you spend it on? I'll repeat that," Miss Palmetto said to Hattie.

Hattie chewed on her lip. "Well, if I had a million dollars," she said slowly, "but couldn't spend it on myself, then I'd have to spend it on somebody else. I'd spend it on my parents, because then they could give the stuff I bought them back to me like presents. Plus, when I got too greedy, 'cause they say I am, they could give the money to the people like over in Africa and Mississippi and right here, too, who need it. Then I could have some and they could, too."

"Hattie, I swear, you can give the darnedest answers," Daddy said, laughing. He jumped up and took another picture, but the flash didn't go off.

Everybody clapped hard and laughed. I heard somebody say, "Now, *that's* a smart child!"

Don't you know I felt some kind of proud, to hear that!

I crossed my fingers again, hoping for Hattie. Miss Palmetto came to the podium. "The judges have deliberated, but before we announce to you who the next Little Miss Ebony Calvary County is, let's have all our contestants take one more walk."

Mary Elouise, Hattie, Libby, Timika, Chaundra, Valerie, and Deidra walked stiffly in a line around the stage. I could see the older girls getting up and taking their things backstage for their turn after intermission.

Miss Palmetto opened the envelope. "I'll start with second runner-up first. The second runner-up for the Little Miss Ebony Calvary County Pageant is Timika Bellamy!"

Timika looked surprised, disappointed, and happy at the same time. She took the bouquet of roses from Billy Weathers, one of the official ushers, while Mary Grant, the current Little Miss queen, handed her the trophy.

"First runner-up," said Miss Palmetto, "is Hattie Stackhouse!"

Bunny and I screamed and hugged each other, jumping up and down. Hattie's mouth was wide open. She grinned then, and grinned again when Billy brought her flowers and Mary gave her the trophy. Daddy had got practically right up on the stage with his Polaroid, trying to get pictures and clap at the same time.

"She did better than you thought!" Bunny said, shaking my arm. "Go ahead, Hattie!" she hollered.

Just then I noticed that Hattie was whispering and whispering to the old queen, Mary Grant, who was shaking her head. Then Hattie turned and stamped over to Miss Palmetto and whispered to her.

Bunny and I froze. What was she doing?

Miss Palmetto spoke into the microphone. "Ladies and gentlemen, I think we should be very, very pleased with this young lady and her concern. She wants her sister Maizell to come out and share her title because she helped her so much. Isn't that grand?" Miss Palmetto began to clap.

"C'mon, Maizell!" Hattie said. "You gotta come help!"

Shyly Maizell tiptoed on stage and took Hattie's hand while everybody applauded and the cameras flashed.

I felt double proud of both of them then. It was like they were heroes, too.

"And now, ladies and gentlemen, the moment we have been waiting for. The new Little Miss Ebony Calvary County Pageant queen is Miss Deidra Washington!"

Everybody began to scream and holler and clap. Deidra put her hands up to her mouth like she didn't know she had won. The other girls crowded around her, congratulating her. Then they all got back in their lines while the old queen placed the crown on Deidra's head.

We scambled backstage so we could get to Hattie as soon as intermission arrived. Momma was smiling and smiling. "Wasn't she wonderful? Wasn't she, though? Didn't she do a good job!"

"And Maizell, too, Momma," I said. "Did you see how she danced!"

Suddenly Miss Wilhemena came around

the corner. "Shhhh, it's not over yet!" she said to us.

When we peeked through the curtains, we could see Queen Deidra taking her victory walk around the auditorium. Her crown sparkled in the spotlights. Then she came back up on stage and stood by Timika and Hattie and Maizell.

Miss Palmetto asked the audience for quiet. "Before we go to our intermission and to the second half of our pageant, where we pick a new Junior Miss and new Miss Ebony Calvary County, I'd like for you to know some history about this pageant. Miz Juanita Weaver Gleason, president of the Calvary County Negro Business and Professional Women's Club, would you come forward, please?"

So Miz Gleason did. She talked about Miz Alfronia Meriwether. She talked about each president of their club. And on and on and on. Hattie and the other girls began to shift around on stage.

"Miz Gleason, sit down!" Bunny whispered.

"In keeping with the tradition of 'Uplift and Uphold, a Better Race and a Better People,' the Calvary County Negro Business and Professional Women's Club has decided to lend its hand to the preservation of historical landmarks in this county," Miz Gleason said, "beginning with the New Africa Missionary Baptist Church Cemetery, where Miz Meriwether is entombed. We will immediately erect an appropriate memorial to her and show that we stand solidly behind the efforts of the community to renovate this landmark."

Several people in the audience stood up and applauded; then the rest of us joined in.

"We also this year created the First Annual Alfronia DeCosta Meriwether Community Service Award as part of our efforts to renovate the cemetery. In future years we will award it to those who have worked diligently to preserve other landmarks. This year's recipient has shown hard work, determination, and commitment in her endeavors to preserve the cemetery."

"Miss Effie, hunh?" Bunny whispered.

"Yeah," I said. "She's gonna be so happy! I can just see all her wrinkles crinkling up in a smile!"

"The recipient of the first Alfronia De-Costa Meriwether Community Service Award, in keeping with our theme of Young, Gifted and Black, goes to Miss Raisin Stackhouse. Miss Stackhouse, will you come forward, please, and receive your award?"

"Raisin!" Bunny screamed. "It's you!"

"What?" I looked blank.

Momma wrapped me to her chest. "Oh, baby, isn't this grand? Get out there!"

Hands pushed me onto the stage. I tried to get myself together as I stumbled toward Miz Gleason. Community Service Award? I hadn't done anything!

Miz Gleason gave me a large envelope, and then Billy Weathers brought out a bouquet of flowers and laid them in my arms. "Thank, thank you," I stuttered to Miz Gleason.

"You're welcome, baby," she said. "Miss Effie said you surely deserved it."

I looked over at Hattie and Maizell, who still held hands. They grinned at me, and I grinned back. Then I grinned out at the audience. I couldn't stop grinning and feeling good.

And the best part about it was that I didn't have to feel bad about not knowing our history because I knew it, at last.

ABOUT
—————— THE ——————
AUTHOR

Eleanora E. Tate is the author of
Just an Overnight Guest,
which became the basis for a film
produced by Phoenix Films, Inc.

The film was named to the
"Selected Films for Young Adults 1985"
list by the Young Adult Committee
of the American Library Association.

Ms. Tate lives in Myrtle Beach,
North Carolina.